Divine
Intervention

Ryan Hussey

ISBN-13: 978-1727834420
ISBN-10: 1727834429

For me.

CONTENTS

ACKNOWLEDGMENTS

I'd like to thank anyone and everyone who's ever encouraged me to keep writing, including my mother, brother, English teachers, and friends—and especially my biggest fans who read earlier versions of this story, some multiple times before I was ready to pull the trigger.

Section One: Fall

1

YELLOW LINES, WHITE LINES

THE RINGING crept closer. Red and blue lights floated until they formed a single line of purple. I couldn't tell if our car was moving forward or if we were still, and everything around us was moving in the opposite direction. A wave of red rushed in and we slowed down. Now the sea of brake lights was purple, too. Everything was. I was drowning in the moment.

I pressed my head up against the rear passenger-side window as we rolled by the epicenter of commotion. I read *ECNALUBMA* on the hood of a red and white truck and giggled as I said it aloud. It was surreal, but it was all so real. I let the moment consume me. We hit a pothole, and I snapped back into it as I noticed two people wheeling a young boy on a stretcher into the back of the truck.

This wasn't the first time I used, and it wouldn't be the last.

Mark kept the wheels extra straight—he always got nervous around sirens, especially now that he was seventeen and had actually gotten his driver's license.

He was the kind of dude who needed to smoke more to chill out but always refused, not because he was against it but because he was concerned with his future. "Then why do you hang around us?" we'd ask. After all, he was a year older. Mark never had a good answer.

A single bead of sweat dripped down the right side of his forehead as the twins cut up another line on his chemistry textbook. I'm sure the half-bottle of oxy in my bag and open handle of vodka on the floor didn't help either.

I saw Mark joggle his head as we passed the lights and sounds, shaking it off like he so often did. Seeing an accident like that was sobering for him—it reminded him that there are greater things at risk when we're reckless, and remembering that helped him keep the wheels straight.

"Aida, you're up." David and Beth passed me the textbook. I'm not like Mark. I like to forget that sobering thoughts exist.

TWO DAYS later, I read about that accident online. A drunk driver had fallen asleep at the wheel and veered into an SUV, forcing both vehicles into the divider. The bastard got off easy, with a few bruises and scratches, a broken wrist, and minimal damage to his car: busted headlight, broken mirror, smashed up door.

They say you're more likely to survive a crash when you're drunk, because your body is more relaxed or something. Like, you don't tense up when you anticipate impact because your reaction time is impaired. Or maybe because you're too intoxicated to anticipate the impact in the first place. It's kind of shitty, but that's the way it happens.

The family in the SUV lost everything. Their car flipped, totaled. Glass everywhere. The husband broke his nose and the wife suffered a concussion from slamming the back of her head on the headrest. She was wearing her seatbelt. Their two-year-old son, Gavin, was the boy on the stretcher. He was in his car seat, strapped in as safely as he could've been. He died at the hospital.

Gavin was my dad's name. I say *was* not because he's passed away but because I no longer speak to my father. I decided not to keep him in my life once I realized I wasn't a priority in his. From when I was a little girl, I felt like he didn't want me around, like I was getting in the way of him and my mom. He didn't think I was his child, and maybe I'm not. But that's no excuse to not treat me like a human. We're all God's children, right? I'm not going to feign spirituality, but my mother is the closest thing to a saint that I'll ever believe in for dealing with my father. It just so happens she's also the patron saint of choosing shitty men.

My family used to go to church every Sunday morning, the normal charade:

Dad wakes up a half hour before Mass begins, hung over. Mom is awake and knows he's going to start getting everyone ready so we can get there on time, but she pretends to be asleep on the off chance he doesn't. I listen to the entire thing from my room, also pretending to sleep. I hear Dad groan and stumble into the bathroom to pee. He half-asses washing his hands and tries to get Mom up. They debate over whether or not we should attend Mass today. Once the yelling stops, I know to get dressed.

The three of us would walk into church about twenty minutes late, treating the marble floor like a minefield— each step carefully planned in advance, making sure none of us made a spectacle of ourselves. We'd tiptoe far enough toward the altar to realize there were no open pews, probably even more embarrassing than showing up late in the first place. God literally had nowhere for us to sit at his house. We'd retreat to the back of the room with the other fake Catholics and stay until Communion.

Standing room was practically reserved for people like us at our church, the Church of Immaculate Conception. We'd stand amongst the same poor slobs every Sunday morning, and though we never spoke to them, it was understood we were from the same mold.

One man was always holding a baby—and this went on for years—as if his wife would pop out a kid and then nine or ten months later, BOOM, there's another one. I guess that's what happens when you don't believe in contraception. Another woman's lipstick was never quite on her lips completely, kind of like she slipped back into last night's dress in whoever's apartment she woke up in and then scrambled her way to Mass. She was a trainwreck of a person who I bet had a hell of a childhood, but she was unapologetically herself, even in church.

Sunday Mass standing room taught me how to people-watch. You know how we observe strangers and give them back-stories? Church is the perfect place for that. You can just look at someone and pretend to know her whole life: her deepest fears, the car she drives, her taste in music, why she used to attend Mass with her husband but doesn't anymore. I understand the irony of people-watching in church, but sometimes it's fun to judge books by their covers. Other times, it's a necessary shortcut.

Once the priest started serving the Eucharist, my mom would give us the nod and we'd duck out the back doors of the church. The ride home was reserved for two conversations: planning where we should go for brunch and adding chapters to the stories of fellow standers.

This was a typical Sunday for me, since as far back as I can remember. As together as my family seemed at Mass, we grew further and further apart over the years. We stopped eating dinner together every night and my dad started coming home a few hours later than usual. Then one Sunday, he didn't round up the troops for church.

I usually kept quiet to maintain the illusion that I was asleep, but that morning I tossed and turned to make noise and attract attention. I even got up to pee and did a pass by my parents' room to see if there was movement. Poking their door open ever so gently, I caught the sound of my dad snoring and knew we probably weren't making Mass or brunch. There he slept, far to one side of the bed with one arm thrown behind his head, what seemed like miles from mom, whose body draped off the opposite end.

MY FATHER left when I was thirteen. His alcohol problem took a nosedive as I reached the last few years of elementary school. Toward the end, his substance abuse manifested itself as physical abuse toward my mom, but that stopped quick after she pulled a knife on him. There's only one other instance I can think of, but it was much more than abuse—he basically tried to murder her. One night on his way home from the bar, my dad saw a woman he thought was my mom on the sidewalk. So, in his drunken stupor, he drove his pickup onto the curb to try to run her down. Luckily, he missed the poor woman and only took out a mailbox. He claimed he slipped on a patch of ice, but there was a good reason my mom refused to walk with headphones in her ears from that point on.

My mom went through a handful of men after my dad. First, there was Pablo. She even learned Spanish for him. "Uno mas, uno mas," she'd say, begging him for another kiss before he left for work. She was happy with him.

Pablo was a truck driver. He did mostly local deliveries, transporting goods from long-distance shippers to local distribution centers. Sometimes he'd even bring home damaged items from the shipments—I actually got a bunch of nice clothes that way. The clothes themselves weren't always damaged, just a tear in the packaging or something. Now that I think about it, I'm not sure how legal it all was. But my mom was convinced it helped Pablo and I connect, so she never said a word. She'd just smile.

Then Pablo left, inexplicably. They always seemed to. I thought I'd be more beat up about it than I was. But the only things I missed about him were the free clothes and my mom's smile. Truth be told, most of her men were interchangeable. After Pablo, there was Roger. He was a writer. After Roger, there was Dean. He owned a restaurant. After him, there was Troy. They all seemed to have douchebag names, too.

Roger was depressed and a little too into pills. He was frustrated because he loved writing and admired the works of Hemingway and Faulkner and Vonnegut, but he knew he'd never be as good. You know, that frustration of loving something so much but being fully aware you'll never excel at it. Roger took his frustrations out not on my mom but on himself. Threatened to jump off a building when he was high a few times—I think my mom found him vomiting in his sleep once or twice. He was lucky to have her.

Being around Roger and my mom made me realize how lucky I was to have her, too. About a month after he took off, I tripped over a curb and broke my ankle. My mother drove me to doctor's appointments and school, sat through my surgery, picked up my pain prescriptions, and cooked every meal for me while I was recovering. How do you leave a woman like that? Someone who gives everything she has to make you happy, to make sure you're okay—someone who is there to take care of you even when it means not being able to care for herself. I couldn't leave her. I never moved out for that very reason. I couldn't live with myself knowing I'd left her alone like some guy would.

By the time my ankle healed up, my mom had met Dean. He sucked. Dean spent so much time at his restaurant that I barely got to know him. He wasn't around for too long. I think he may have liked the idea of my mom more than he actually liked seeing her. He never made it a priority to learn my name, and whenever he was around for dinner, the restaurant had a kitchen fire or a chef called out. "If you want something done right, you've got to do it yourself." That's the one thing I learned from Dean.

I'm not sure he realized what a dangerous lesson that was to teach a sixteen-year-old. But even though I didn't care for him, Dean had managed to show me how to take control of my life. With this inspiration, I went through a drastic transformation during my sophomore year of high school. I cut my signature long, black hair to about shoulder length and dyed the tips purple. I pierced my nose, first with a stud and then switched to a ring. And since I didn't have the money to buy all new clothes, I started wearing only my torn black jeans, band tees, and a black zip-up hoodie that I'd stolen from a Pac-Sun. Defining my own look was my version of control.

In the midst of my metamorphosis, my mom started bringing this dude named Troy around. Troy was an interesting character—a bit younger than my mom but still double my age. Him and I bonded over music. He used to bring his acoustic over and play songs as we both sang along in the family room. He made sure he knew my favorite Nirvana songs.

What else could I write? I don't have the right. What else should I be? All apologies. It almost felt like a family again.

Troy used to tell me I had a beautiful voice. I knew he was saying that mostly to be nice, but I can sing in key, so there's that. He asked me to sing backup for him at a gig once. It was a dive bar with a small crowd—maybe fifteen, twenty people, tops.

Women were giving him the eyes. He was a little bit drunk, so he was giving them back. Troy was mostly harmless, so I thought nothing of it at first. But then I caught him during a break, getting too close for comfort with some slut in a strapless red top and black hooker boots. I confronted him about it on the way home from the bar.

"You don't know what it's like," he defended himself.

"What, having a handful of trampy fangirls eye-fuck you the entire night until you finally choose the lucky winner?"

Troy pulled the car over. "No." He took a deep breath and didn't make eye contact. I had no idea what he was about to say, but I knew it was going to make me look at him differently.

"You don't know what it's like, Aida," he began. "I am in love with a great woman who gives me everything I need. Yet, I feel empty. I feel like, on another level, I'm missing something important—like I'm doing something wrong even when I know I'm not."

About a week later, Troy packed up and hit the road. My mom thought she'd pushed him away when in reality it was mostly my fault. That night after the gig, he kissed me in the car. He didn't try anything else inappropriate because, deep down, I believe he was a good guy. But he and I both knew he had to go.

I spent weeks wrestling with whether or not I should tell my mom. Telling her would've made her hate Troy, and maybe even track him down and threaten to press charges that I'm not even sure would hold up. It would've also hurt our relationship, though I'm sure she'd've finally seen me as an adult. Troy did, and maybe that's what endeared him to me. Of course, not telling my mom would've kept her believing she was the reason he left.

In reality, Troy needed to figure his own shit out. When you get into a relationship with someone a little older, things seem refreshing at first. You're able to see everything from a new perspective. But after a while, it can mess with your head. He needed time to grow up on his own.

My mom loved Troy the most out of all her boyfriends—maybe even more than she loved my dad. That's exactly why I never told her about what he'd done. Sometimes, it's better not to know all the details, to keep your version of a loved one intact.

2

A SECOND CHANCE

Remember not the former things, nor consider
the things of old.
Isaiah 43:18

I BELIEVE in a higher power. I believe in forgiveness. I believe in treating others the way you want to be treated. I may not believe in every word of the Holy Bible, but I do believe God has some sort of plan for everyone. Not necessarily predetermined, but I believe that everything happens for a reason.

I believe in people. I see the good in the world, through random acts of kindness every day—people going out of their way to help strangers in need. During my missionary work, I've witnessed a child, no older than six or seven, stop in the middle of his soccer game to help an elderly woman fill her bucket at the well. I helped put that well there to provide clean water for the village, but I'd like to think I had nothing to do with the child's unselfish behavior. It seemed innate, as if the boy walked over to that well on instinct alone, like he realized he had a purpose in this world that was larger than himself.

Simply put, I am a man of God. I was not always spiritual, and I, too, have my faults. But I believe this world is a better place when we all put our faith in something. It doesn't have to be God—it could be anything. I'd be satisfied if we just put our faith in each other, at the very least.

A person who believes in nothing is dangerous, terrifying even. People like that have nothing to lose, nothing to keep them grounded. They cannot be forgiven because they do not feel remorse. But I believe these people can be reinvented. I believe they can be introduced to faith, given something to believe in, and forced to have an open mind. I don't mean against their will, but everybody needs a little push to change sometimes. I believe these people can be saved.

I also believe in second chances. God knows, I've had mine. But resistance to change is human nature—we are mostly creatures of habit. To overcome this hesitance, we must encourage each other to get better, to do better. Because sometimes, with that little outside push, humans can do great things. All men and women have the potential to be great, but many struggle to find the motivation to do so. Some of us need experience tragedy so we can locate this point of light within ourselves.

I WAS nine years old when I lost my mother and have been a churchgoer ever since. My father was always a heavy drinker, but even more so after my mother got sick. It was his coping mechanism—and his crutch. Going to church, though, was his idea. Since the only way he could explain my mother's cancer to me was as "an act of God," he figured it was only right to confront Him on a weekly basis.

And so we drove into Philadelphia every weekend to attend Mass. But while my father went to St. Elizabeth with the hopes of finding answers, I found something better: faith. The most beautiful thing about faith is that you don't need to see to believe. You trust that everything happens for a reason, that it's all part of some master plan God has.

My father had trouble coming to

grips with that idea at first. It took him several months to curb his drinking. He knew it was something that had to be done once he noticed my interest in the Church. That's when it all seemed to click for him. Alas, his point of light—that motivation that drives men to do great things, to exceed expectations. A second chance.

After two years, my father was completely sober. He attended all the meetings, did all the exercises, completed all the steps. I was so proud of him. By then, we'd become full-fledged members of the Catholic Church. We attended Mass every Sunday morning—sometimes even Saturday evenings—and we gave donations when we could afford it. At one point, he was working three jobs: daytime mall security, overnight shifts at a trucking company warehouse, and construction jobs on the weekends with one of his buddies. He was lucky to get four hours of sleep some days. But we always found time for Mass.

We helped organize canned food drives for Thanksgiving, volunteered at soup kitchens for Christmas, and participated in at least two or three church retreats a year. Most dads bond with their sons over sports or cars; my father and I became closer than I'd ever imagined because of the Church. While some of those dads watch their sons grow up to be professional athletes or lawyers or run the family business, my dad watched me become an ordained priest. And he was proud of me for it.

He was there for almost every sermon I gave, sitting toward the front, captivated by every word I spoke from the altar. One day, I noticed he wasn't at the church. I scanned the pews and even the standing areas in the back, but I didn't see him. After Mass, I swung by his apartment to find him on the floor next to his couch. My immediate fears quickly subsided, as I found no bottles, cans, or flasks in his apartment.

My father regained consciousness in the ambulance, telling me the last thing he remembered was going to sit on the couch and dropping to the floor instead. At the hospital, a young-looking doctor told us they'd administer some tests to see exactly what was wrong. I planned to sleep by my dad's side that night, but he insisted I go home to get some rest. Early the next morning, I received a phone call.

The doctor spoke softly over the phone, with the same soothing voice she'd used in the hospital. But something about her inflection was different. It felt off. Practiced. It felt as if this was the first time she had to tell someone his loved one had an inoperable brain tumor, and that they'd start radiation treatment immediately to try to shrink the cancer. Optimistically, my father only had about a month or two to live.

THREE MONTHS came and went, and although my father fought his illness courageously, he passed away on a Wednesday. I remember that because it was Ash Wednesday. I kept to myself for almost two weeks following his death, only leaving my apartment for the liquor store and his funeral, the same scene replaying in my mind.

"I'm glad we did this," my father mustered up.

"You're going somewhere nice," I said, tears running down my cheeks. "I love you." Using my father's hand, I wiped a tear from my face. I felt a weak squeeze from his hand, his way of saying, 'I love you, too.'

I buried my father on a gloomy Saturday, rain falling on and off. You'd think he hadn't any family at all judging by the turnout. I'd done my job and contacted every living relative of ours, as well as old friends of his whose phone numbers hadn't been changed. I had even used Facebook to get in touch with a few of his buddies from the Boy Scouts.

Some responded, some didn't. Some lived on the other side of the country, so I didn't expect them to travel all the way to Philly for a man they hadn't seen in decades. Only about ten to fifteen people showed up.

Perhaps the most important trait I got from my father was his open mind. He had this unwavering desire to see a situation from every angle, and worked to understand everyone's point of view. Because of this, he was never hesitant to try new things. Even if he didn't necessarily agree with something, he'd make sure he gave it a shot before claiming it wasn't for him. This is how he was when we'd first gotten involved in the Church. He'd put up a little bit of resistance, but he'd usually come around.

My father's objective nature was not the only thing I inherited. Prior to his death, I could count the number of drinks I'd had in my entire lifetime on two hands. Once he got sick, I not only became distant and disillusioned—I became him.

I didn't realize it was a problem until I returned to the church to celebrate Mass. Admittedly, I held several Saturday evening Masses with a little more than a buzz. The issue wasn't that I was incapacitated—but that I was functional. By being fully capable of performing my duties at Mass, I didn't acknowledge the fact that I had an actual problem. It also made it tough for other members of the church to recognize what was happening behind the scenes. Aside from getting a decent whiff of my breath, there was practically no way to know I was intoxicated.

This went on for almost two years. I tried to stop but couldn't. I'd have two or three good days in a row, followed by one really bad one, where I couldn't stop thinking of my father or couldn't stop seeing my mother's face in a crowd of parishioners. Searching for that light within myself, every door I opened led to another dark room. Lonely, desperate for something positive—I spent most nights in my apartment with just God and a bottle. I talked and talked and talked to him, but He never answered back. Part of me began to wonder if He'd ever answered. Had I just tricked myself into believing these were two-sided conversations all along?

How could there be a God who does this to somebody twice in one lifetime? Blessings are sometimes disguised and we cannot prepare for most events in life, but why would a benevolent God do this to me again? A man who'd given up so much and still remained loyal to his faith, a man who'd lived through one tragedy after another—*why?*

Everybody has their own problems to deal with, but as a spiritual leader for so many community members, I couldn't afford to focus energy on mine. The weight of others' issues combined with my own became too much to handle. With the pressure at unbearable levels, my only escape came in liquid form. That sweet solace of catching up with an old friend— Jack, Jim, Johnnie, whomever else was available on any given night. These folks made me feel a little less lonely, even if it was just for a few hours at a time.

I AWOKE one night in a hospital bed, head pounding. I had no recollection of how I got there or what angel saved me from whatever situation I was in. All I remembered was being frustrated that I was almost out of bourbon, and all I knew in that moment was that something needed to change. I had this overpowering feeling that—whether I liked it or not— God was about to step in and turn my world upside down. Change was inevitable, and I'd better adapt quickly.

"You're lucky to be alive," the doctor told me. I didn't believe in luck.

Up until then, all that talk about finding a point of light within ourselves had been conjecture. Both rehearsed and ad-libbed words came out of my mouth during sermons, and those words made sense. People connected with them, believed them. Don't get me wrong, every word I spoke was genuine. But when I looked around my hospital room and wondered how I'd gotten to that exact moment, I feared that my words had been uninspired.

I couldn't go back to the church—not right away, at least. I needed to find my point of light again. I needed some time to myself, to escape the prison my addiction had forced me into.

When the time was right, I packed all of my essentials and left for Burundi. Missionary work had always been an interest of mine, but I'd become too invested in my local community to leave. I wanted to help churchgoers with all of their problems and give back as much as I could to the Philly area, but my hospital bed realization forced me to see the rest of the world differently. There were places that needed me. People may assume I was running away from my issues by heading to Africa, but the way I see it, I was running toward something bigger.

Some of us need tragedy to catalyze change and improvement. Others need it to ignite a desire for betterment in the first place. My problem had been lying dormant all along, and only after losing both of my parents did I recognize it. Tragedy triggers pain, pain incites a need for change. Sometimes, we must overcome unthinkable adversity to locate the path to righteousness.

3

THE ART OF USING

I WAS seventeen years old when I first ventured down the rabbit hole. It started with the occasional bump or two, nothing serious. Like, if I took a weekend trip to the Jersey shore with some friends, we'd make sure we had enough to hold us over, you know? But then it got worse.

I had little to no money to begin with because I helped my mom pay rent. My newfound addiction didn't help the cause. Some months, I contributed next to nothing. One month, I got arrested and my mom needed to bail me out—so I contributed less than nothing. Mom barely made the rent.

I felt like shit because she worked so hard to raise me right and make up for my dad leaving. That's one of the reasons she'd try to get serious with her boy-friends so fast. She wanted me to have some sort of father figure in my life, even if I was already a teenager. And at the same time, she knew a loving boyfriend would chip in to help us keep the apartment. For some reason, none of them ever tried to get us to move into his place.

My mom wasn't the only one dating, though. I knew that if I was going to help her afford rent, I'd either have to make more money or spend less. I chose, well, a version of that: a loophole in the form of horny teenage boys. I didn't have to make more money if I was spending less of my own. It's amazing what lengths a boy will go to get what he wants. And don't label me a 'tease' either—I knew exactly what each guy wanted and I gave it to him, eventually.

Everyone was happy. The boys got stories to brag to their friends about, I got shoes and art supplies I'd never be able to afford otherwise, and my mom and I got to stay in our apartment. These boys also helped fund what was becoming a bad habit of mine. Part of me felt guilty for dragging them down with me, while an-other part of me knew it was their own faults. My mother raised me well enough to know what I was doing was wrong, but not well enough for me to stop doing it. It's wrong to use people, I know that. We live in a world that's *use or get used*, though. I'd rather some naive momma's boy with a few extra bucks be broke for a month than my mom and I be homeless.

Using people became one of my greatest skills. I learned how to play on others' emotions, how to manipulate people into reacting the way I wanted them to. I mastered the art of making others feel sorry for me, and I took advantage of the 'damsel in distress' archetype. I sought out people who went out of their way to help others in need, as if it were some type of spiritual high for them. Their kindness often ended up in a more corporeal high for me. I used people to survive. I used drugs to live.

MY FIRST time was like an indie horror film—poorly lit, awkward breathing in between the unappealing sounds of human flesh rubbing against more human flesh. You've seen the movie: A boy with too much hair and cologne ends up leaving a party with a girl who's had too much to drink. They head to his car and drive around the block to an empty parking lot. He loses his shirt, then hers, then their pants mysteriously go missing, too. No background music, no artistic montage, no budget—just one long take of teenagers trying to recreate what they'd seen so many times on the internet and HBO.

The kissing is sloppy, the foreplay nonexistent. There's some lip biting because that's what he thinks she likes, based on the porn he's watched. Her bra doesn't come off on his first try or second. She has to remove it herself. Neither of them had ever used a condom before, so safe sex becomes a fleeting thought in the pitch-black back seat of his 2003 Ford Focus. The experience as a whole is short-lived, especially the main event. Thirty seconds, tops.

I woke up the next morning in my own bed, feeling like a completely different person. I felt grown up, like I had aged a decade overnight. Hung over, yeah. But this new feeling—the feeling that I was in control of my body—made me crave it more. I itched to feel that way again. I began expressing myself in this physical fashion more and more frequently. Sex made me feel independent. It made me feel powerful.

The partner didn't matter. I didn't do it for them; I did it for me. It was a selfish act, and once I realized I could get even more out of it, I used it to my advantage. I didn't have to feel guilty for doing something I enjoyed. But I couldn't use that mindset for everything.

I may not have experienced guilt when I slept with randos, but I did feel guilty every time I got high, however brief. Guilt was a perfunctory reaction when it came to drugs, at least for me. I'd feel like I was standing on a thin slab of ice and everything around me was falling, but after a split-second, the feeling would go away. I've always been able to shrug it off and get past that roadblock to bliss. Getting high made me feel mature and childishly innocent at the same time. Drugs gave me strength, like Popeye's spinach. They made me feel almost as invincible as sex did.

The freedom I had, to do what I wanted with my body and my time—that helped me withstand the labels people threw at me. Slut, whore, tramp. Druggie. Burnout. Teenage girls are afraid of things they can't categorize. So, when I didn't fit nicely into one of their stereotypes, they invented all new labels to brand me as something they could understand. But that was exactly the problem: they could never understand me.

They didn't know my past and never took the time to ask about it. Ignorant to my motivations, they couldn't grasp why I acted the way I did. They'd rather assume I was nothing like them.

I WILL never forget the day I lost my mom. I was twenty. It was sudden—the way you wake up from a bad dream, except I wasn't dreaming. Reality was the nightmare. I envy those who get a month or two's notice about their parents' terminal illnesses. They have time to think, time to prepare. They have time to say goodbye and maybe even hello for the first time. They know what's coming, so they're expecting the inevitable, and they know enough about it to come to terms with the fact that it's inevitable.

I didn't have that luxury. Many claim they wish their parents had died in a more sudden manner, so they didn't have to watch them suffer. The thought of a long, drawn out process pains them, as if the body and mind had begun decomposing right before their eyes. The slow death of a loved one is not something I'd wish upon anyone, but I'd give anything to have just one more day with my mom.

She collapsed one day in the kitchen, as she was cleaning up the dinner table. I immediately called 9-1-1 and rode with her in the ambulance to the hospital. She never spoke another word. She'd had a stroke, essentially making her a vegetable for the few hours she had remaining. I sat by her side in the hospital bed, reading magazine articles to her and pleading with her to wake up. She never did.

My mom's stroke occurred on the left side of her brain, meaning that—had she woken up—it would've affected the muscles on the right side of her body. Even though she was unconscious, the right half of her face looked droopy. It reminded me of the way an ice cream cone melts, but I never said that out loud. There was really nobody to say it to.

Nurses came in and out to check on my mom—and me, I guess. But nobody attempted to start conversation. They noticed how bummed I was, how utterly destroyed my entire world seemed. Who wants to rile up the sad girl? Leave her be. If I were less heartbroken at the time, I would've tried to contact some of my mom's old boyfriends. There's no guarantee any of them would've shown up, but I'd like to think someone other than me would've visited her in the hospital.

My mom never kept in touch with the guys she used to date. All were clean breaks from the tree of her life, the fallen branches gathering around the trunk in enough of a pattern to tell a story but not enough to capture any meaning from it. That being said, they all showed up at her funeral. Every last one. It was almost as if they'd had a club or something. Weekly meetings, organizing fundraising events to afford renting a bus for everyone to attend the proceedings. I'll never forget how awkward it was when they all realized exactly what each one of them was doing there.

I was the daughter in mourning, clearly. But then there was a random assortment of men just kind of standing around, no one to comfort them and no one but me to console.

Once everyone realized what was going on, it became funny. All half-dozen men or so bonded over stories about my mom—nothing too inappropriate, just ridiculous things she did over the years. Some stories, I knew. But others, I was hearing for the first time.

I'd never heard the one Pablo told about her leaving the remote in the fridge. She wanted to watch TV while he was on a route and actually called him to accuse him of losing it. After twenty minutes of arguing, she went to pour herself some cranberry juice. Sure enough, there the remote was, on the refrigerator door right next to the ketchup. The best part was that she immediately ended the call without admitting wrongdoing, and let Pablo believe he was the one who'd misplaced it. She finally came clean the next time the remote went missing and Pablo found it in his sock drawer.

Dean opened up about how he'd met my mom. She was out to dinner with friends at his restaurant and was so unhappy with her scallops that she'd sent them back to the kitchen and asked to speak with a manager. Dean came out and calmed her down by offering to cover the entire table's meals. Since she was the only single woman of the bunch, one of her friends decided to leave my mom's number on a napkin with a note that said: "Dean, call me." And when he did a few days later, she had no idea how he got her number and accused him of stalking. I think I laughed for ten straight minutes at that one.

But while these stories gave me a reason to smile and remember the good times, the memories only made me miss my mom more.

After leaving the cemetery, a bunch of us went back to the apartment. My intermittent staring into the distance made the guys feel so bad for me that they decided to throw a little impromptu party, even though there was nothing to celebrate. Surprisingly, it wasn't weird being back in our home—my home, now—with more than one of my mom's exes. And once we all got a few drinks in us, I actually enjoyed their company. Dean, Paul, Roger, Pablo, Eddy, Troy. We had a good time.

THINGS ESCALATED as the night went on. We drank, smoked, sang, danced, laughed, cried a bit, then laughed again. When I started cutting up a line on the coffee table, the guys decided to call it a night. Each gave me a drawn-out hug and told me everything was going to be okay—that he'd be there for me if I ever needed anything. As the group left, I grabbed Troy's hand and asked him to stay a little longer.

"I'm not sure that's a good idea, Aida." See, I told you he was a good guy.

"But I'm not tired," I pleaded with him. "And I don't know what'll happen if nobody's here with me. I shouldn't be alone."

Troy looked at me, half-knowing I was taking advantage of the situation, half-knowing I was right. I could see him doing the math in his head: All of the other guys had to be up early the next morning for work. They had responsibilities. Shit, two of them even had wives and children. Troy knew he had nothing important going on in the a.m., so it made the most sense for him to be on Aida watch.

He came back inside, insisting he'd stay for a bit, but only until I fell asleep. His guitar was leaning on the edge of the couch. I handed it to him and asked him to play me my mom's favorite song.

The first few notes were enough to bring tears to my eyes. I instinctively took the coke out of my pocket and dropped some on the table again. Troy stopped playing.

"I'm not letting you do that to yourself," he said. "This is why I stayed."

After looking up for a second, I ignored him. He put his guitar aside and knelt down next to me. I closed my eyes and a few tears trickled down my face—but I was too numb for them to be real. Troy may have stopped me from doing more drugs that night, but I was going to get the high I craved whether he liked it or not.

"Is it?" I said, looking him in the eyes. Wiping the forced tears from my cheeks, I kissed him to see how good of a guy he actually was.

4

SAVIOR

I know that you can do all things; no purpose of yours can be thwarted.
Job 42:2

I RETURNED from Burundi in autumn, a fresh start for me. Instead of being the beloved priest who left his loyal parishioners at St. Elizabeth, I was the interesting newcomer at St. Anthony's. The church community greeted me with open arms. The welcoming celebration was humbling. About a hundred parishioners and diocese members gathered with homemade food and desserts. They even made sure that nobody brought alcoholic beverages.

When I came back to Philly, I'd been sober for almost three years. For this reason, I offered my time to help run the church's weekly AA meetings. Naturally, people came and went in this group, with plenty of folks attending just one or two meetings before vanishing. I managed to strike up a friendship with a young man named Evan. He was a United States Army veteran wounded by an IED in Iraq. Evan had lost the lower half of his left leg in the explosion, along with two of his fellow soldiers and closest friends.

He returned stateside to his girlfriend, but it wasn't long before he stumbled down a disastrous path of alcoholism and domestic violence. She left him and his life began to spiral out of control. He stopped talking to his family and refused to show up for his 9-5 data entry job, resulting in financial problems and a brief stint of living on the street. Knowing he needed to make a change, he showed up at one of our meetings.

I made it my short-term goal to help Evan find the light within himself, that motivation to do better and be better— something he hadn't felt since he'd signed up for the armed forces.

St. Anthony of Padua is the patron saint of lost things. When I was younger, at the peak of my father's faith, we used to have a statue of St. Anthony in the house. If anything went missing—my father's wallet, a piece of jewelry that used to belong to my mom, the TV remote—we'd kneel down in front of St. Anthony and pray that he'd help us find it. Usually, within days, whatever was missing would turn up.

I'd like to think I arrived at St. Anthony's in Philadelphia exactly when I was supposed to. Using the church's AA meetings as a platform, I shared my experiences with alcoholism to provide hope to people like Evan. I left a few details out, of course—but the truth to the story is never what's important. It's the lesson behind the narrative that matters. That's what sticks with people. That's what inspires them to change or think differently.

EVAN CAME to three or four meetings before missing one. During those first few, I spoke about habits: how to identify when a behavior becomes habitual, and how to distinguish positive behaviors from negative ones. I also discussed how these behaviors affect other people. There comes a point in the battle with substance abuse when you need to consider your loved ones and your community. Just because you don't interact with someone on a regular basis doesn't mean you don't have an impact on that person's life.

Continually performing a negative behavior may make that habit seem okay for people who look up to you. I explained this to Evan in brief conversations after each session. He hung around to thank me, and I gladly connected with him more deeply—to make sure my message was getting through to somebody.

When he didn't show up one week, I worried I wasn't getting through at all. I was afraid I'd failed—that, even with the extra focus on my part, Evan was destined for relapse. I'd assumed, as was the case with so many of his AA brethren, the program had ultimately failed him.

But it hadn't. Two weeks later, he came back.

"I was worried we'd lost you, Evan," I said, approaching him after a meeting.

"No, sir," he replied. "I was in Arizona." He called me *sir* often.

"What's in Arizona?" I wondered.

"My mom." He cleared his throat. "Well, my mom was in Arizona," he said. "She passed away last week."

My heart broke for Evan. Here was this sweet young man who'd already been through so much—and more of a hero than I'd ever be—experiencing yet another loss. Some of us are built to withstand this type of damage over and over again, but others shudder at the thought of death, especially if we haven't grown accustomed to it. Very often, people who've lost parents and other loved ones at a young age are more equipped to deal with loss later in life. They know which parts of themselves to turn off, and which emotions to experience freely.

Before I could offer Evan my condolences, he added, "I had a drink on Friday with my brother—it was for mom—but that was it. Haven't even thought about having one since."

I assured him it was fine. People deal with loss in different ways, and Evan seemed to be the type that was comfortable with death. He almost had to be. He'd been surrounded by it for the better part of a year when he was overseas.

After the meeting, Evan explained that his mother's death had brought him and his brother closer. They knew they needed each other now more than ever, and their longtime feud no longer seemed to matter. What did matter—love, family, relationships—outweighed the trivial reasons they'd been avoiding one another for so long. Evan and his brother realized that neither of them had a legitimate excuse to be distant. Sometimes, it takes a death for us to appreciate life.

WITHIN THREE months, Evan's path seemed clearer than ever. He found a well-paying chef job at a chic Center City restaurant. He'd always loved to cook, majored in culinary arts in college before enlisting, and had been working in a kitchen since he stopped drinking. His younger brother, Jimmy, moved his family from Arizona to a small town in south Jersey—only about a half hour from Philadelphia.

One week, Evan informed me he'd no longer be attending meetings. He insisted he never felt the urge to drink anymore, and I trusted him. I could tell in his eyes that he had the strength to resist even if he had the urge in the future.

Since I wouldn't see him at meetings, I encouraged him to come to Mass every once in a while. As someone who stands in front of large groups of people on a regular basis, I notice when familiar faces are missing. I jokingly warned Evan, "Nobody's keeping track, but I'll know if you skip a week."

When I look out during Mass and see faces I don't know, I begin to form stories in my head about how they got to this very moment. What brought them here, to my church, during my Mass? Was something I was about to say going to change their lives?

Sometimes, I see a new face but it's not there the next week, or the week after. I wonder what would make someone come to a service one time, but not return. Did I turn them off to St. Anthony's, or were they just in town on a visit? Have I turned anyone off to Christ altogether?

Evan came to one service—it was a Saturday evening, and I remember that because I figured he'd be working at the restaurant on a busy weekend night. My sermon was about temptation: how you're always going to feel tempted to give in to vices or to compare yourself to others—but when you recognize temptation for what it is and overcome it through God, you experience true power and autonomy.

When I didn't see him the weeks following, I didn't want to believe he'd given in to temptation. I prayed he hadn't. Evan now lived a life to envy, with much to lose: a job he loved, a brother he'd reconnected with, three beautiful nieces, and an adorable nephew.

One weeknight, after sitting in on a substance abuse meeting at the church, I ventured to Evan's restaurant for dinner. As the server walked me to a table, we passed a transparent divider, through which we could see the kitchen. Slicing, seasoning, sautéing—it was a mesmerizing, organized chaos. I requested to be sat facing the kitchen, so I could see Evan at work. After perusing the menu, I watched through the divider as the server relayed my order to the kitchen staff. But I didn't see Evan. When my server passed by again, I waved him over.

"Hi, this is a lovely restaurant," I said. "I've heard such good things and can't believe I haven't been here before."

"Thank you," he nodded. "How can I help you?"

"Are all of your chefs working tonight? I came to see an old friend named Evan. Does he not work here anymore?"

"Did you say 'Evan'?" The server's smile faded.

"Yes, but I don't know his last name." I felt silly. "You see, I'm a priest at St. Anthony's in Chestnut Hill, and Evan used to come to—"

"Sir," the server interrupted. Ironically enough, he had addressed me just as Evan would've. "Sorry," he said, searching for the words. "Your friend was a wonderful chef...."

EVAN HAD died the Sunday prior in a freak accident. As he was making a left turn on his bike, an eighteen-wheeler's brakes failed and the truck struck him in the intersection. Tragic, yes. But it was more deflating than anything. In his

Philadelphia Inquirer obituary, which I burrowed into my garbage can to find, his brother claimed Evan was on his way to church when the accident occurred—not St. Anthony's, but his new church, closer to where he lived on the other side of town.

Almost immediately upon leaving the restaurant that night, I turned to throw up in a trash container. I'd taken my meal to go, but it wound up in the same place as my lunch. I couldn't bear to carry that box of food home, and I no longer had an appetite anyway.

When we feel overwhelmed, it's common to revert to old habits. I wouldn't call it temptation—I'd describe it more as instinct. If we're not used to dealing with a specific situation, our minds and bodies handle it in a way that's familiar. Even if it's one of those behaviors we've worked to change, instincts kick in to get us back within our comfort zones.

For situations that are all too familiar, many of us experience the same sort of phenomenon. We intrinsically react in whatever way gets us back to homeostasis—be it an old habit, family tradition, or something completely unique to us. For me, old habits and family traditions are synonymous. Any attempt to restore balance in my life inevitably ends with me peering into the soul of an empty bottle, questioning why I don't feel any different than I did when it was full.

This time, my instinctual reaction led me directly to a liquor store. My plan was unconscious, but simple: Leave the restaurant, get home, and drink myself into a coma—or until I forgot who Evan was and why just saying his name was enough to evoke the deepest level of sadness I'd allow myself to feel. But plans get derailed. I never made it home with the bottle.

On my walk home, I heard a whimpering sound coming from an alleyway. I passed by cautiously, peeking into the darkness to find its source; I'd assumed it was a feral cat. As I neared, the sound stopped. I tiptoed closer to its origin to discover a person lying on the ground. It was a young girl, no older than her early twenties.

I froze.

"I'm going to get you help," I assured the girl, and reassured myself.

When the EMTs arrived, she was completely devoid of life. Motionless, pale, with dried up foam outlining her mouth. I rode with her in the ambulance and slept in the waiting room of the hospital that night. I wondered how long she'd been in that alleyway, and how many people passed by before I had.

At the hospital, an emergency room nurse told me I may have saved the girl from an almost-certain heroin overdose. I told her, "We all have our vices," knowing full well I'd abandoned mine in a dark alley somewhere in North Philly.

5

SAVED

TO COMBAT my numbness, I look for thrills. Ironically enough, when I turn to things like coke and pills for these thrills, I become even more numb. But when I use people for a buzz, it enables me to feel something—even if it's just temporary.

My whole life, people have worried about leaving me alone. *What would happen if we leave Aida by herself? What if she starts feeling lonely? Would she end up hurting herself?* Truth is, I get into more trouble when I'm surrounded by people. If I'm alone, there's only so much I can do—and I assure you, the possibilities are no worse than what I could do with someone else thrown into the mix.

When I woke up the morning after my mom's funeral, Troy was already gone. I expected him to be, and it doesn't upset or disappoint me when people act in a predictable way. Actually, I prefer the predictable—that makes it a lot easier for me to control situations.

But something was different about that morning. It was the first time I didn't want to be left alone. It was the first time I worried for myself—and the first time I *had* to worry for myself. I longed for company: Troy, my friend Mark, anybody. I found myself beginning to feel again, and I was having none of it. As a parting gift, Troy made sure he took my stash with him, so when all I wanted to do was desensitize, I had no choice but to feel.

As the hours passed, I sat in different rooms of our apartment. My apartment, now. No matter how hard I tried, I couldn't bring myself to think of it like that. Every change of scenery made me realize how surrounded I was by my mom. In each room, I noticed more things that reminded me of her—evoking specific memories, some of which I forgot were even there. Photos of birthdays, holidays, spontaneous weekend trips to the beach. Each one unlocked a story I used to love transporting back to.

But now, I wanted them to disappear.

Every last one. I'd had enough feeling for the day, and I needed a break. I needed to start fresh.

WAKING UP in the hospital isn't as exciting as it sounds—especially when the one person you call for and want to see is six feet in the fucking ground. When I came to, the nurse made sure I knew who I was, where I was, and what had happened. She told me the doctor wanted to speak with me, but that they'd let me rest a bit before she came in.

I saw a man in the hallway. White guy, maybe in his 40s or 50s. He had a full beard: well-groomed, but with speckles of gray. I could tell he'd been through some shit. He looked tired, like he'd had just as rough of a night as me. I didn't know who he was, but I had a strange feeling I was about to learn a whole lot.

"Who's that?" I asked the nurse, pointing to the man outside my room.

"We believe he saved your life, Aida." I shook my head. "When you're ready, I can let him come in here so you can talk."

"But I don't know him."

The nurse looked at him before responding. "He's a priest...."

"Why is he still here?" I said.

What did it matter that he was a priest? That meant nothing to me, and

frankly, I was uncomfortable knowing
that he'd been wandering around the
hallway and waiting area, pacing back and
forth while I was unconscious. Even if this
man did save my life, I didn't need to trust
him. I didn't need to speak to him. I didn't
need to listen to whatever silly, pseudo-
philosophical self-help shit he had to say,
and I definitely didn't owe him a thank
you.

Did I?

"I can ask him to leave if you'd like,"
the nurse offered.

I paused. In that moment, I realized I
didn't have anybody to come see me at the
hospital—nobody who knew I was there,
and nobody who would care enough for
me to call for support. No family or
friends to show up in hysterics but stay
strong for my sake. Nobody to tell me everything was going to be all right, and
make sure I got home okay. Not Troy,
Mark, the twins—these were all shallow
relationships, because that's how I'd designed them to be. Every relationship I've
ever had was based on what I needed
from the other person. I've never really
known how to form a friendship based on
mutual respect and compassion. Or love.
If someone wasn't going to help me get
what I wanted, that person was of zero
use to me.

Then I thought, *Would they even show up?* If I called someone like Mark or Beth or David, would they even pick up the phone? I found solace in my certainty that Troy would be at the hospital in a heartbeat, but was that really what I wanted? At this point, it wouldn't be fair to him. Because I'd made him feel like he owed me something.

So, maybe it was okay that this priest stranger had taken my safety into his own hands. Someone clearly had to. I sure as hell wasn't prioritizing it, and the least I could do was thank him and find out why he had no better place to be.

AFTER SPEAKING with the doctor, it was clear I wasn't getting out of that room for another day or two. Now that they knew the circumstances surrounding my near-overdose, no nurse or doctor trusted me. They tried to get in touch with estranged family members, but nobody even showed up at my mom's funeral—so why would they suddenly haven given a shit about me?

My mom had two sisters, both older. One lived in Utah for some reason, and the other was kind of a rolling stone. She'd lived up and down the East Coast, and I think she'd settled somewhere in Canada—but who knows for how long?

My mom had a brother, too, but he died
when I was eight or nine. I don't remember him attending any holiday get-
togethers or birthday parties, and I can
count the number of times I've seen my
aunts on two hands.

For now, that strange man standing
twenty feet from my hospital room was all
I had. I figured I'd humor him, to see
what types of inspirational, existential
stuff he'd say. Maybe he was full of shit,
but maybe he wasn't. I never could tell
with priests. Their faith never seemed to
waver, but I used to be able to tell when
one was having an off day. They are
human, after all. We all have off days.
Sometimes, you question whether your
beliefs make enough sense to preach them
to other people. Sometimes, you do
enough heroin to almost numb yourself
permanently.

I asked the nurse to invite the priest
to speak with me. When he walked in, I
could tell he was probably having not only
an off day but an off week. I remembered
priests always smelling so clean—as if
God had bathed them himself. But he
smelled like shit. God hadn't drawn this
guy a divine bubble bath in days.

Okay, I knew he'd rescued me from
an alleyway and he'd been patrolling the
waiting room for like eighteen hours, hop-

ing I'd survive... But was that a good excuse to look and smell homeless?

"Nice to see you awake," he said, sitting down next to my bed. "I'm happy to see you're doing better. I've been out there praying for you."

I had nothing real to say, so I forced a smile and faked a cough. After an extended silence, the priest cleared his throat.

"Sometimes, we do things for specific reasons. They're calculated attempts to maintain or alter the status quo. And sometimes, doing something drastic and doing nothing at all feel like one in the same."

I found myself captivated by the way he spoke—priests often had that effect on me when I was younger. I didn't know if I agreed or disagreed with his message yet because I hadn't fully processed what he was saying, but I was absorbed in every word.

"Other times, though," he continued, "it seems as if our actions have no meaning. But they do. We might not realize it in that moment, but a motivation deep, deep down drives us to act, or not to."

I sat there silently, listening without letting our eyes meet.

"Sorry. What's your name?" the priest stopped to ask.

I turned my head toward him, finally

making eye contact. "Aida," I mumbled.

"Aida, I don't know you, and I don't know what happened in your life to drive you to..." He paused and exhaled slowly through his nostrils. "I don't know how you ended up in that alley last night, but I believe I was there for a reason. And I'm here now for that same reason: I want to help you."

Looking away again, I shook my head. Why would this stranger want to help me? How could he? I've manipulated everybody I've ever allowed to get to close to me—and those relationships began and ended on my terms, usually leaving the other person with a terrible taste in his or her mouth. I'd never been helped because somebody wanted to help me. I didn't want this priest's help, and God knows, I didn't need it.

THE PRIEST left the hospital after about twenty minutes of speaking. I hardly said a word while he was in the room. I felt humbled by him, unable to get full sentences out in his presence. Before he went on his way, he wrote down some information about his church—and invited me to stop by for a service or if I wanted to talk again. As soon as the door shut and he was gone, I knew I probably wouldn't take him up on his offer.

The hours passed, scraping on like weeks. I couldn't sleep. The priest said he didn't know what had happened for me to end up where I was, but I wondered what had to have happened for him to actually want to help me. I understood that his type naturally wanted to improve people's lives and encourage a more righteous way of living. But there were plenty of troubled young people in Philly who were much more worthy of his time.

Besides, he'd already done enough for me. He went out of his way to call an ambulance, then he spent an entire day making sure I survived, and I didn't even remember to thank him. If I went down to that church and wasted any more of his effort, I'd just add to the burden he'd placed on himself. Then, next time something happened to me, my suffering would become his—and that's not fair.

One thing the priest said stuck with me, though. After I'd managed to string together a group of words into a semi-coherent phrase, he shared his take on loneliness.

"I've never felt so completely and utterly alone," I said, to some extent.

He asked me if I'd meant *alone* or *lonely*. I didn't see a difference between the two. He explained that lonely is just a feeling, but alone is a status. You can feel lonely, but you can be alone. Lonely is usually temporary, fleeting. You have no control over it. Alone is often a conscious decision—a situation you've created for yourself, whether you've intended to or not.

Thinking more about it, I believed I meant *alone*. It was something I'd felt, but it had a permanent vibe to it. I wondered if he was implying that I was the architect of my own loneliness.

For a man who knew next to nothing about me, he had a pretty decent idea of who I was—and what to say to get through to me. But I didn't let him know that, through reaction nor response. As far as he was concerned, he may as well have been talking to a wall.

Section Two: Rise

6

WILLING TO CHANGE

*Therefore we do not lose heart. Though outwardly we are
wasting away, yet inwardly we are being renewed
day by day.*
2 Corinthians 4:16

EVERY FEW weeks, I stopped by
Evan's grave to pay my respects. There
were always flowers at the foot of the
headstone, which I assumed his brother
replaced frequently because they never
appeared faded or dying. Each time I visited the gravesite, I'd also notice four
small rocks sitting on top of the memori-
al: one for each of Evan's nieces and one
for his nephew. This is commonplace in
cemeteries, as flowers and notes seem to

disappear over time—either with the wind or the graveyard maintenance crew.

When my father and I used to visit my mother's grave, I'd try to find the most unique-looking rock in the vicinity and place it on her headstone. However, the cemetery staff would always remove it by the time of our next visit. After a while, I ran out of rocks that excited me and began placing handwritten notes. I figured, if whatever I placed on my mother's grave was going to be taken away anyway, I might as well make it something personal and important to me. I wondered if Evan's loved ones would learn to do the same.

He was flawed, yes, but we all are. What I admired most about Evan was that he was willing to change. He'd promised himself that he'd improve, and he made a legitimate effort to abandon his most destructive behaviors. Was he changing the world? No, but sustainable solutions start with one person at a time—a slow, steady progress toward a better future.

I didn't overcome my addiction in a day. Neither did Evan, and nor will Aida. That was her name, the girl from the alley. As I sat in the hospital waiting room, praying she'd wake up so I could talk to her, I realized what God was doing. I had made a positive impact on Evan's life, and due to an unfortunate accident, he'd never get to see the fruits of his labor. But God was not done with me—He knew my influence could help another lost soul, searching for meaning.

I believe He placed Aida in that alley for that reason, so I could find her and help turn her life around. God didn't want me spending time mourning the loss of a friend. He needed me to get back to work—His work—and spread the lessons I'd learned through my own mistakes and experiences.

While I paced the hallway outside Aida's room, I chuckled to myself. I was sure, to an outsider, it would seem like damaged individuals are projects to me. Evan might be an unfinished one, a project for which I'd never get to measure results—and Aida, a new and intriguing challenge I'd embrace with an open mind. But I've never viewed people as projects. As rewarding as it is to help another person realize his or her value, I gain nothing but happiness from watching people overcome obstacles on the path to a more virtuous life.

I genuinely hoped the girl would find her way to St. Anthony's. While I knew I could guide Aida toward the life she deserved to live, I wasn't positive she even wanted my help in the first place.

68

"A SECOND chance is a terrible thing to waste," I said, beginning my homily. It was a Sunday morning, but this Mass felt different than most. "After succumbing to temptation in the Garden of Eden, God awarded the human race a second chance. That opportunity for reconciliation came in the form of His only Son, Jesus Christ. He was sent to our world to absolve us of our wrongdoings, to die for our sins. Temptation, however, was 'not of the Father.' As John writes, temptation is a worldly construct. It was created to test the strength of our beliefs—to muster up the courage and power to rebuke evil and stand on the side of all that is holy and good."

I looked out into the pews and noticed what I said was resonating with most people. I hoped that among the nodding heads I'd see Aida.

"But overcoming temptation is never easy. It's not designed to be easy. If anything, it's gotten more difficult over time. Adam and Eve were tempted with an apple from a gorgeous tree. Lord knows, many of us face more temptation than that before we leave the house in the morning. But temptation does not equate to sin. Jesus lived without sin His entire life, but did He experience temptation? Of course. He was no different from us in that respect. However, we can find our own triumph in His victory over sin—and let His overwhelming defeat of temptation serve as inspiration when we're feeling the most conflicted."

After Mass was over, I stood by the doors of the church to thank parishioners for joining me in what felt like a powerful, cathartic service. A young woman approached me, nervously smiling.

"Good morning, Father," she said.

"Perfect way to start a Sunday, no? And I got you out of here just in time to grab some brunch and catch the Eagles game."

"I was hoping to stick around and talk a bit," she replied. "I never did thank you."

That's when it clicked. I hardly recognized Aida, which I realized was foolish, as if I was expecting her to still look as unkempt as she did after nearly dying. She was, in fact, a beautiful young woman. On this Sunday morning, she looked nothing like I'd remembered, which was the most uplifting sign one could hope for. I invited her to stay as long as she needed to, to talk about whatever was on her mind.

WE SAT in a random pew toward the front of the church. Well, the pew I'd selected may have seemed random to Aida, but there was one particular row I liked to sit in—I considered it the best seat in God's house. Four rows back from the front on the right side, with a spectacular view of the altar and a direct angle to my favorite stained glass window, featuring an angel that had always reminded me of my mother. It was a straight shot across the church from another breathtaking mural of angels, and if I turned my head around, I had an unobstructed view of the humbling, symphonious organ.

I often sat in that pew when I needed to feel powerless. It was a nice break from the pressures I placed upon myself on a daily basis. The spot let me know I wasn't in control of everything—that, although there were some aspects of my life and others' lives I could influence, many important things were completely out of my hands. And perhaps it was better that way.

Once we settled into my preferred pew, Aida appeared nervous again. Her eyes wandered around the church. Sure, there were plenty of distractions, but I couldn't help but think the true distraction was internal. She wouldn't hold eye contact with me for more than a second, and she made it clear she wouldn't be the first to speak.

"When I was—" I cleared my throat and took a deep breath. "I lost my mother when I was nine years old. It wasn't until then that I became religious." Now that I was talking to her, Aida directed her focus to me. But she remained unresponsive.

"My father and I attended Mass every week after she passed away," I continued. "Whether we needed someone to blame or to make sense of what had happened, I can't remember anymore. But whatever it was kept our attendance consistent."

Aida mumbled something.

"I'm sorry?"

"How did she die?" Aida said, speaking up. "Your mother." Now it was me who couldn't maintain eye contact, for fear of breaking down into tears. How ironic that would be, while trying to help another person overcome her own traumatic experience.

"Cancer," I replied. "It was cancer."

"Did you get to spend time with her before she died, or was it sudden?"

Aida's candor caught me off guard, but I found it oddly refreshing. "She had a few months—both of my parents did, actually."

"I think that's better," said Aida. I stayed quiet so she could expand. "It's fortunate—I mean, it's unfortunate to have your mom or dad die—but I think it's fortunate to be able to spend time with them when there's an end in sight."

"What makes you say that?"

"What if there's something you really want to say to them? Or something they've always wanted to do that they've been putting off? You can help make those things happen, knowing that it'll be one of the last memories you have with your loved one."

"If you're waiting that long to say or do something, there's probably a deeper reason," I challenged her. "Why wait until a loved one is on his or her deathbed to be truthful and transparent?"

Aida nodded her head in agreement, then said, "What was the last thing you remember your mother saying to you before she died?"

"I was young—"

"You don't remember?"

"I don't know if it's exactly what—"

"What was the last thing she said, Father?"

"'I love you.' She said, 'I love you,' and squeezed my hand." On the verge of tears, I looked down at my left hand and squeezed it with my right, just the way my mother had the last time I saw her.

"See, you remember it because your mind prepared for it," said Aida. "And it's something beautiful. It's a moment that will always be with you, even if your mom's not."

I'd never opened up like this to someone I intended to help. I used my personal experiences to provide insight into life lessons I'd learned—or to illustrate Bible passages, but I rarely spoke about my parents. With Aida, though, quoting the Bible seemed pointless. She wanted something real from me, and even if I hadn't planned to talk in depth about my childhood or my mother, that's what she was getting.

What I hoped would be a conversation about consistency—and keeping promises we've made to ourselves and others—turned into a Q&A about my past. I didn't mind too much, but I wanted to stay focused on Aida, so I could find the driving force behind her behavior and give her applicable, actionable advice.

"Tell me more about you, Aida. Do you live with your parents?"

"I lived with my mom up until recently," she replied hesitantly. "She, uh, died the week before you found me."

I didn't know how to respond. I'd assumed something disastrous caused her whole world to come crashing down, but this... This made me wonder if Aida's substance abuse had been a long-time habit or an isolated, reactionary incident.

"Aida, I'm so very sorry for your loss. So, you've been living by yourself?" I avoided using the word *alone*. She nodded. "What about your father?"

"My dad? He left when I was barely a teenager. Haven't spoken to him since." Before I could dig deeper, Aida continued, "We were close when I was little. We actually used to go to church every Sunday, too—as a family. Were we the best Catholics? No, not by any stretch of the imagination. But we were together."

I let the sentiment linger, then asked, "Have you reached out to him since your mother passed? Does he have any way of knowing?"

Aida brushed the thought aside. "I don't care if he knows, and I don't think he'd care. That piece of shit—" She quickly looked up at me. "Sorry, Father..."

"It's fine, Aida," I assured her. "Much worse has been said within these walls, I'm sure."

"It's just... I hate drunks. I know I have my own problems, but my life is better with him out of it."

"I understand why you feel that way, but—"

"He was a drunk. A worthless drunk disguised as a decent guy for years, but that's what he always was under the surface. And he used to hit my mom when he got really bad. So, she kicked him out, thinking he would come back a changed man—or at least a man willing to try harder. But he never did."

"Do you think he deserves a second chance?"

"No," Aida replied.

"And you? Do you deserve one?"

"I think so."

"What makes you say that? Why doesn't your dad deserve another chance to find his way, but you do?"

"Because I'm trying."

7

THE RIGHT TRACK

AS WE pulled up, I felt like I was in a faraway land—like some *Wizard of Oz* shit. It didn't feel like Philly anymore, at least not the Philly I knew. So many odd-looking trees, with wind chimes hanging from them, all making the same noise. I stepped out of the car and it sounded like the chimes were whispering, "Turn around," signaling this wasn't where I was supposed to be. It wasn't, but I'd brought this upon myself.

Everything was so white. And not like avocado toast–, Garth Brooks–, board games–white. White like the actual color; everything looked so clean. The outside of the building was spotless, the benches on the lawn immaculate and rust-free. Had I fallen into an alternate reality? Or was I dead, walking up toward the pearly gates to await judgment?

As I glanced around the front of the building, I noticed an eerie sense of calm. When the breeze died down and the chimes shut up, I experienced what I initially assumed to be true bliss. Part of me thought I'd be chasing that feeling for the rest of my life. Another part of me knew it was my fight-or-flight response—and my consciousness caught the first plane the fuck out of there.

What I may have mistaken for bliss was a new type of numbness for me. It was more extreme than any lack of feeling I'd had when my mom passed away. People always talk about having out-of-body experiences, and that's what I was living. I was completely aware of my surroundings but physically unable to react. I was on autopilot.

"Aida, are you okay?"

The priest had taken the ride with me because he knew I had nobody else. He spoke to me about second chances and rejuvenation for basically the entire drive. Our driver stayed quiet, somehow not picking up on my telepathic messages to change the subject or hit a pothole to derail our conversation.

According to the priest, I was being

awarded a rare opportunity to show myself, the world, and God what I was made
of—to overcome adversity and my own
doubt. To be reborn.

My numbness wouldn't permit me to
answer his question. Was I okay? I sure as
hell didn't know, and I was in no condition to speak for myself. I managed to
shake my head, so not to make any rash
assumptions about my wellbeing. But no
words came out of my mouth. The priest
stepped in front of me and we stopped
walking, about ten steps or so from the
door.

"You don't have to do this if you don't
want to, Aida." He was being sincere.
Granted, I didn't know him super well,
but I could tell he'd take me back home
without a second thought if I said I wasn't
ready. He continued, "But I do think this
is the best thing for you right now. And I'll
be here every step of the way."

His support was reassuring, yeah. But
was I really about to check myself into
rehab?

I DIDN'T get to choose what type of
treatment program I enrolled in—the
priest chose for me. He'd chosen the
place, too.

The priest had spent an entire night
researching the best rehab centers in the

Philly area, or so he said. He also told me if I committed to the inpatient program and spent at least three weeks at the treatment facility, the church would cover the cost. I desperately needed that to happen, and I desperately hoped it would work. Finally, proof that those weekly donations go to a decent cause.

I wanted to get better. Did I think an outpatient program—one that didn't require me to live at the treatment center for a few weeks—would've been sufficient? Of course. But if that didn't work, I'd be back at square one. Or worse: end up in the hospital again, or dead.

I was no longer indifferent toward death. The idea of dying kind of scared me, and I wasn't going to give up however many years I had ahead of me for a pointless high. The problem was that, even though my mindset had changed a bit, my body still wanted the drugs. Apparently, that's how addiction works.

Before the priest left me to it, he tried to give me a hug. Caught off guard, I flinched. I didn't mean to offend him, but I felt extremely out of my element, and I couldn't feign things like emotion, optimism, patience, or kindness.

"Aida, I know you don't know me very well, and that's okay. I just need you to trust me. Trust yourself. Trust this process. And most of all, trust God's will."

I looked up from the floor at him. He continued, "If God didn't want you here, believe me, you wouldn't be here right now." The priest broke eye contact and looked out the window. "And neither would I."

That last statement confused me. Did he mean God saved him? Or that he wouldn't have been standing in a rehab facility if he hadn't stumbled upon me—a chance encounter that only happened according to God's will? I felt like it was one of those things where I should've known exactly what he was saying, but I was thinking more into it than necessary. Maybe my misunderstanding was a product of my situation. After all, my state of mind was fragile and in disarray. I decided to let it go, and the priest left with a simple, friendly wave.

Once he was gone, I expected the facility staff—a group of faceless, scrub-wearing nematodes I could only refer to as *them*—to drag me out of my room and begin to torture me with experimental techniques. For some reason, I was under the impression the priest had taken me to a mental hospital rather than a rehab center. I didn't really see or understand the difference until I'd been inside the walls for a day or two.

Most people who opt for residential treatment programs are pretty normal. A lot of the patients I met were just like me—drug addicts, yeah, but folks who lost their way and were looking to get their lives back on the right track. Some knew what their right track was, others didn't have a clue. But everyone had one thing in common: whether they wanted to be there or not, each person knew they had something or somebody to live for.

This woman Alexa was addicted to meth. She had three kids and still found time to get high. She told me she wanted to be clean before her youngest child was old enough to know what was going on. The eldest two already hated her, she said.

Marty was a parent, too. Lost his daughter to some rare bone disease and then got hooked on pills. Wife divorced him and left with his infant son, and his family excommunicated him.

I wasn't sure where I fit in. I didn't want to be there, but I knew I had to be. Trying to identify my right track was a headache-inducing nightmare. Everybody I had to live for was long gone, including the Aida I'd once loved and respected. The role I'd so often played with an apathetic smirk didn't seem to suit my circumstances anymore. And as I sat there, alone, in my new room, I realized that my jagged, contrarian nature had been more of a mask than a testament to my true self.

TO START my treatment, I met with a young, attractive clinical psychologist. He was probably in his early thirties and he had a sort of sexy salt-and-pepper thing going on with his hair. He wore old man glasses, which I found charming in a way, albeit unfashionable. After I sat down in his office, he closed the door and introduced himself. I assumed this formality would soon be followed by what normally transpires in cheesy pornos or those weird erotic novels:

The doctor sits down in his chair, mere feet from the couch I'm sitting on. He tells me to make myself comfortable. Taking his hint, I inch closer toward him and place a hand on his thigh. The dialogue at this point is background noise— the words don't matter as long as facial expressions and eyes combine to tell the real story: that our mutual attraction was too much to overcome. Sure, he tried to remain professional, and I wanted to get better, but God's will be done, our bodies were like magnets.

"Hi, Aida," he interrupted my fantasy. "My name is Dr. Monterro. But you can call me Jason." I nodded and folded my arms. "Is it chilly in here? I can raise the temperature if you'd like..."

"No, I'm fine," I said.

"Okay then, let's get started." He went on to describe something called cognitive behavioral therapy, a goal-based psychotherapy treatment that approaches problem solving in a way that makes sense for the patient. Basically, Dr. Monterro was going to help me identify the underlying reasons I felt certain ways, and empower me to challenge and change those attitudes to shape positive behavior. Sounded great, in theory.

"Depending on how we progress over the course of the next month," he explained, "we'll determine whether or not we need to keep meeting every week." While I found myself smitten with the doctor, these appointments weren't something I wanted to keep doing once I got out of rehab. Suddenly, I was focused and driven—I think.

"So, Aida... Tell me about your parents. What was your childhood like?" I didn't want him to go there, but I remembered it was his job to go there—to force me to dig deep and let myself experience the pain, so I could pinpoint the root cause of my problems. So I could single out what was driving me to act irresponsibly, and overcome it.

During my first session with Jason, we discussed how I knew what I was doing had a negative effect on my life and those around me. But what I couldn't figure out was whether I kept doing it because I felt invulnerable, or because I truly didn't give a shit about what happened to me. I sure as hell didn't feel so invulnerable anymore.

When I walked out of Jason's office, I felt at least twenty pounds lighter. I even smiled at people in the hallway. I wasn't convinced this sensation was a direct result of speaking with Dr. Monterro, but I made sure I enjoyed every second of it—because it was the closest I was going to get to a high for at least a month, and hopefully a lot longer.

I was excited to finish my treatment and get involved in the church—to become part of an actual community. I'd never really done something like that. I briefly joined yearbook club in high school, but the advisor asked me to quit after I'd slept with all three boys on the staff. According to Ms. Sieman—which was a horribly ironic last name—I was causing too much trouble, and it was leading to fights amongst the team. Me, trouble? No way.

Obviously, I'd never told the priest that story. But regardless, those days were behind me. On this journey toward recovery, I wasn't only giving up the substances that had crash landed me in rehab. I had also given up sex.

Quit cold turkey. Took a pledge of abstinence—not officially, but I'd essentially slipped on an old chastity belt and thrown away the key. Even if Dr. Monterro made a pass at me, I'd politely decline his advances. As awesome as that sex scene would've been, I knew that, if I was going to make a change, I needed to change all of my negative behaviors—not just the ones that were illegal.

Contrary to my expectations, rehab was not torture. Granted, I went through withdrawal for about six days before I'd even gotten to the facility. That kind of sucked. It was like the flu but worse: non-stop sweating, intermittent chills, and I couldn't stop shitting or feeling like I had to shit. What my body needed was water and food, but what it wanted—what *I* wanted—was a high.

And that's what they don't tell you about detox: it's more strenuous psychologically than it is physically. I'd had the flu before, and withdrawal was nothing I couldn't handle. But the fear that those symptoms were permanent, that I'd never escape the feeling of always having to shit—that doesn't subside right away. My whole body feeling broken, figuratively and literally, wasn't something I wanted to live with. And that's where depression comes in. If constant pain, nausea, and needing to vacate an already-empty stomach was going to define my existence, I wanted to cease to exist.

During that awful week, I thought about killing myself nearly every day. How easy it would've been, me alone in the apartment, surrounded by plenty of sharp objects. But I was too weak and sick to even attempt it. And by the time I could muster up the strength to entertain the idea for real, I didn't feel so shitty anymore. People don't kill themselves over the flu.

Luckily, by the time I got to rehab and had to talk out my many problems with Dr. McScrewMe, my body had detoxed from all the trash it'd been used to. The suicidal thoughts lingered for a while but soon vanished. For some reason, I was pumped to get out and establish myself as a productive member of society.

The real world terrified me, though. What if I went back to my old ways?

In the center, there were no outside pressures—just me, my thoughts, and a supportive group of people: Alexa, Marty, doctors and all. But out there, beyond the center's white-ass walls, was everything that had driven me down the path to self-destruction in the first place. Stuff to drink. Or smoke. Stuff to snort, swallow, inject.

I was resolute not to venture down that path again. Relapse is the end result for nearly 50% of people who struggle with drug addiction. I promised myself and Dr. Monterro that I'd do everything in my power not to become just another statistic.

8

OUR OWN PRISONS

*Walk with the wise and become wise, for a
companion of fools suffers harm.*
Proverbs 13:20

DURING THE month Aida spent at
the rehabilitation center, I developed a
church-sponsored program specifically
for young recovering addicts. I wanted
there to be a process in place for her—a
soft landing spot once she completed her
treatment. At the same time, I saw her
situation as an opportunity to help other
afflicted young men and women. I also
hoped that the St. Anthony's community
would serve as an 'off-ramp' outpatient
support group, and I couldn't wait to

equip Aida with the tools she needed to tackle her toughest challenge: discovering who she was in the world post-addiction.

For so long, harmful substances were how she coped. They eventually, and inevitably, became a part of her personality. I hoped that, through her treatment, she learned that any substance or behavior she'd been addicted to was not who she was—and that the only thing that defined her was how she acted, especially in times of great adversity.

I believed in Aida. I wanted her to succeed, and I'd spent many of my waking hours planning how I'd help her assimilate into our parish, and praying that she'd be strong enough to resist temptation. One thing that made me feel guilty was the only lie I'd told her. She was under the impression that St. Anthony's was covering the costs of her rehabilitation treatment, but the church had nothing to do with it. We didn't have that kind of money—and especially not for a single, non-parishioner's recovery.

I didn't want Aida to feel indebted to me in any way. As I guided her through this process, I simply wanted her to feel inspired and encouraged and for her to show her gratitude by keeping the promise she'd made to herself.

During my time at St. Anthony's,

we'd never welcomed a soul like Aida into our family. I preached to essentially the same group of people every Mass, with new faces sprinkled in here and there. That was part of the reason I started organizing support groups and recovery meetings at the church. They gave me the opportunity to interact with an entirely new variety of people—and to actually make a difference in their lives.

See, most of the Mass regulars didn't need my convincing or support. They believed in God, and just made it a habit to show up every week. Others kept coming to services because they thought it was required of them.

But religion shouldn't seem like a moral obligation. In an ideal world, people pray and attend Mass because they want to feel like they're part of something much larger than themselves. There's a communal aspect to faith, and then there's the inspiration to be better, which comes from meeting people at Mass and other church events. Those shared experiences give us insight into how others see the world—and I believe everyone can benefit from communicating with both like-minded individuals and people they don't necessarily agree with.

When I first spoke with Aida the day after I found her, I could sense we didn't agree on everything. In fact, we probably didn't agree on most things. But I could also tell, through some ephemeral warmth that came over my body during our conversation, that her and I agreed on perhaps the most important thing: that people can change.

"I FEEL like I'm in jail," Aida said, with a touch of panic in her voice. "The white walls... they make this place feel like just a really clean jail cell."

"Aida, it's fine." I didn't know what else to say. Sometimes, we trap ourselves in our own prisons—these cells we feel ourselves confined in are usually our own doing. "Remember that it's only temporary."

"I know, I just don't know if I can get through this."

She'd only been at the rehabilitation center for three days, so I was confident she would settle in and flourish. My faith in people wouldn't allow me to believe otherwise.

"You made it through withdrawal with nothing but sheer willpower, didn't you?" I suspected the Lord had something to do with it, but she deserved all the credit I could give her.

"Ugh, the worst experience of my life." She let out a deep exhale. "Thanks,

Father. Happy to have someone on my side."

There was no telling how long Aida would last in treatment, or how strong her willpower actually was. I hadn't known her that long, and though I wanted to put all of my faith in her, I had my doubts.

"Hey, do you think we can make this, like, a regular thing?" she asked.

"What do you mean, speaking on the phone?"

"Yeah, I'm gonna need someone to talk to on the outside." We shared a chuckle. "I was thinking maybe once a day?" When I didn't answer immediately, she clarified, "If that's okay with you, of course."

I knew this was my chance to fully invest in Aida. Everything I'd done up to that point was significant, but the idea of daily conversations seemed like a true turning point. A lot of commitment on my end, but who else did she have, really?

"That sounds fine to me, Aida. Are you sure you won't get sick of me?"

"I can't promise you anything."

"Well, promise me this," I said. "That you'll keep trying—"

"Father, of course I'll keep trying," she interjected. "I want to be me again. Just me. Nothing more and nothing less."

"When was the last time you'd say

you knew who *Aida* was?"

"I don't know," she searched inwardly for an answer. "Probably when my dad left."

She hadn't let me finish my sentence earlier. What I wanted her to promise me was that she'd keep trying to forgive her father. With rebirth often comes understanding and compassion—and with that, Aida might be able to reconcile with the man who had given up on her and her mother. Even if she never saw him again, this exercise would be useful for her in the long term. He'd been a major catalyst, I suspected, in her teenage undoing. And once she overcame her addiction, she might also free herself of whatever animosity she felt toward this man.

I blamed God for my father's death at first. For me, He was the one I couldn't bring myself to forgive. Many drunken nights were spent talking to a wall, or a ceiling, or a painting. There was one specific portrait I'd speak to in my apartment, one my father had left me. I knew 'The Son of Man' was a pretty famous piece of art, but something about it made me think it represented God.

To me, God was the essentially faceless man in the painting, with His eyes discreetly watching me from behind a green apple. So, in a sense, He could see me but I could never fully see Him. His face would always be obscured by this piece of fruit in front of it—the very fruit that represented temptation in the Bible. The apple hovered there in a seemingly random fashion but precisely concealed the part of God I wished I could recognize, so I could blame a specific face for everything wrong with the world. And my life.

For Aida, the anonymous man in the painting would be her father. She couldn't fully see him, but that didn't stop her from blaming his absence for all of the hardships she and her mother faced.

"DOES IT still feel like prison?" I asked, before giggling, "Not that you should know what prison feels like."

"No, it feels like college now," Aida replied. She'd been in the center a week. "Not that I'd know what college feels like either."

She described the group of people there as a community, not unlike what you'd find on a university campus—just on a much smaller scale. People came and went, but the dynamic never changed. And when someone completed the program, it was celebrated as a 'graduation' ceremony.

"So tell me about the outside world..."

"What, you guys don't have windows there? Television? I know they take your phones and tablets, but they must let you watch movies and TV."

"We get movie nights and a few of us will watch the Flyers games."

"Oh? How are they doing?"

"Not too hot this season. I guess you're not a hockey fan?"

"My father used to take me to games, but I was always more of a baseball and football guy. Hockey just never did it for me."

"Was it the fights? A lot of people get turned off by the violence."

"Football is pretty violent." I laughed at the memory that surfaced. "My dad took me to an Eagles game at old Franklin Field when I was—oh, had to be nine or ten. And, if you haven't noticed by now, Philly fans are tough."

"That's putting it mildly," Aida laughed.

"Well, it had snowed and the Birds were tied up at halftime after throwing a really bad interception. So, this rent-a-Santa comes out—I think it was actually a fan from the stands—as part of a Christmas show and—"

"You were NOT at that game."

"You've heard the story? I guess most people know it. Basically anybody from here and most football fans."

"Did you throw one?"

"Of course not."

"I don't believe you."

"Aida, I was nine! Even if I'd made a snowball, there was no way I was reaching the field."

"Mmhmm."

"If I could hit Santa from that distance, I would have been in uniform and not in the stands."

I REMEMBER one night in Burundi, I awoke to a faint tapping noise. It sounded like it was coming from right outside of my room. Unable to see a thing, I felt around for my flashlight, swearing I left it beside my bed. Nothing. Then I heard what sounded like a page turning.

As I cautiously poked my head outside, I scanned the nearby area. To my left, silence. To my immediate right, a small boy sitting on a bucket, holding my flashlight and a book he must've taken from my bag. He was silent too now, wondering if he'd done something wrong.

"It's okay." He offered me the book back. "No, you keep it. You seem to enjoy the pictures."

I sat down next to him as he re-opened the book and flipped through the pages to find the illustrations. It was a book about Philadelphia—I'd picked it up in the airport before leaving the States. I loved it for the same reason the boy did: wonderful depictions of the Philly skyline and scenes like Valley Forge, the Liberty Bell, and Market Street.

The boy went from picture to picture, unknowingly tapping on the edge of the book when he enjoyed one. Each time I noticed his reaction, I tried to explain to him what the scene was like in real life. Of course, he didn't understand most of what I was saying, but sometimes human connection transcends language. Sometimes, we connect in spite of language and the barriers created by it.

When we got to the Philadelphia Zoo, the boy was mesmerized. Bright colors, smiling faces, and dozens of families gathered around a lion exhibit. But the concept of caged wildlife confused him. He didn't seem to understand tourists either. As I attempted to convey the essence of a zoo, the boy pointed at the two lions in the drawing.

He was confused by the cage and wanted to know why these creatures were confined. Had they done something wrong? Were they being punished? To him, nobody really owned wildlife; that's why it's called wild. So, why would people gather around to watch these majestic wonders of nature trapped in a cell?

I reasoned, perhaps to myself, that many of the animals in Burundi were accustomed to being around people, and vice versa. In America, lions wouldn't assimilate well into everyday life. Plus, introducing foreign predators would disrupt the ecosystem. The fading flashlight provided just enough illumination for me to catch his body language and subtly furrowed brow, from which I could decipher, "But lions kill—let the lion be a lion."

And, if that's what the boy meant, I'd have to say he was right. What separates humans from lions is that lions have the instinct to kill, to survive. People possess humility and empathy, both of which allow and empower us to change. It just makes a lot more sense to change after we've been kept in a cage awhile.

9

RECOVERY

MY TREATMENT program involved what they called a 'lockdown' policy, which meant no visitors for the duration of my stay. I could, however, speak to the priest on the phone when I wanted to. And I did—once a day, every day. After the first few days, our calls felt like two friends catching up. I'd tell him about my new friends at the center and how many of them were going through the same recovery process I was. He'd offer me some spiritual guidance, then tell me all about upcoming events at the church and how sometimes church politics complicated decisions more than he'd have liked.

The priest tried not to gossip, and he was pretty good about it. "Great minds discuss ideas; average minds discuss events; small minds discuss people," he'd say, as the famous quote went. Sometimes, though, he'd slip and vent about the church's longtime members—they were the most frustrating. The irony was that, while he seemed so hell-bent on my personal transformation, a lot of the people he dealt with on a weekly basis were terrified of change.

"About a year ago, we tried to move the Sunday morning Mass starting time back by a half hour. And sure enough, a few of the—how do I say this—more seasoned churchgoers had something to say about it."

"What?!" I questioned. "How could they not be okay with sleeping in a little later on a Sunday?"

"These people have their routines, Aida. Even a change as slight as a half hour could throw off their whole schedule for the day, or even the week."

"That's so... sad." People with crazy routines always scared me. I understood the importance of consistency, but not being able to deviate from the usual seemed ridiculous. "Life is what happens when you're busy making other plans, right?" I quoted.

"I suppose," countered the priest, "but there's something to be said about the value of plans, too." I knew he was right. "Without plans, you wouldn't be able to appreciate the spontaneous things. That spur-of-the-moment trip for ice cream your parents take you on wouldn't seem as cool if all of the events preceding it were just as unpredictable."

"Okay, but a half-hour shift in Mass time isn't something spontaneous. It's just a change to the pattern that already exists."

"And that's exactly why they weren't fans of it," the priest explained. "If something happens in addition to the routine, fine. If something interrupts the routine once in a while, okay. But if somebody tries to change the routine altogether, all hell is bound to break loose."

"Do you think routines are important for recovery?"

"To an extent, yes." I stayed quiet so he'd expand. "Establishing a healthy routine is great and all, but you have to make sure it's sustainable."

"How do I do that?"

"Let's say you were trying to quit smoking, and all of the people you spent your time with were heavy smokers."

"Oh, okay..."

"You may be doing all the right things and be on your way to quitting, but at the end of the day, you're still surrounding yourself with the temptation to smoke."

"I get that you need to surround yourself with the right people, but isn't that type of temptation good, in a way? Like, shouldn't you be able to resist cigarettes or booze or whatever if you're really on the right path?"

"I guess it all depends on how much you're willing to trust yourself."

ST. PATRICK'S Day isn't the same in rehab. I didn't know you could throw a St. Paddy's party without booze. I mean, I knew that there were recovering alcoholics in the center—and some of them were actually fun without their vices. But isn't the whole point to drink and be silly? Just because there's green and orange clovers everywhere doesn't mean the celebration is up to snuff.

It wasn't until the dry St. Paddy's Day party that I noticed how hypocritical I'd been. How could I claim to have hated drunks but enjoyed their company so much, even before I'd gotten to the center? I loved to drink and bullshit with my friends, all of whom were not-so-mysteriously absent in my life once shit went bad. It was becoming abundantly clear that those relationships had been based on behavior and not on genuine connection. Maybe the only thing we'd had in common was that we liked to get fucked up—and that we were fucked up most of the time.

I enjoyed talking to the priest because, even though my behavior was what originally brought us together, we bonded mostly by discussing ideas. After all, 'great minds discuss ideas,' right? He respected me as an individual—an imperfect one, at that—and he tried to offer guidance even though I knew he'd never been through what I was experiencing.

"Father, I'm torn here... I don't want to ruin people's progress—and I definitely don't want to mess up what I've got going for me. But how do you have a St. Paddy's Day party with Pepsi and seltzer?"

"Aida, what do you expect in a rehabilitation center? It's the best they can do, and it wouldn't benefit anybody to have alcohol involved."

"I know, I know. I'm just saying, why even celebrate then?"

"Well, people celebrate holidays without getting wrecked."

"I guess..."

"Aida, what's really bothering you?" He was good at that. Even over the phone, he could tell if something was up.

"My mom was an enabler."

"Most mothers tend to be. What do you mean, though?"

"She enabled my dad for years, then he left. And when I got into a bit of trouble, she enabled me. I miss her so much, but what would she have done if she were still alive? Would she have made me check into rehab?"

"I didn't make you do—"

"Okay, sorry. Didn't mean to make it sound like that. You know what I mean. Would she have come to the hospital to comfort me and tell me everything was going to be fine? Or would she have made me... change?"

"I don't know that I feel comfortable making assumptions about what she would do. I never met the woman, unfortunately." He took a breath. "But you're talking about rehab as if it's a cure-all. You know that it's not, right?"

"Yeah, of course. But I'm putting in the work."

"The work doesn't stop when you leave that facility, though. It gets tougher out here."

"I know."

"A lot of folks end up back in rehabilitation programs because once they lose that structure, their lives spin off the rails again. And the element of temptation makes staying clean even more difficult."

The priest wasn't wrong. I'd made some friends in the center, but I was careful not to get too close to anyone. It was a strange game of musical chairs, with people coming and going every day. Some would leave on a high note—no pun intended—and cry throughout their graduation ceremony. Those were tears of joy. And accomplishment. Others would timidly nod their way through it, squeaking out tears of hopelessness, giving the impression that they'd wind up back in the center soon and there was nothing they could do about it.

What killed me was that, since I never tried to keep in touch with people after they'd left, I had no way of knowing if they got better. Would they thrive in the real world, or would they just end up back in rehab—or worse?

THREE DAYS. Do you know what can happen in three days? Your cut can scab. The mechanic can fix your car. Those Chia Pet things can start to grow fuzz. Your jeans can wear perfectly. Your goldfish can die. Leftovers can go bad. You can write or paint a masterpiece. You can read a whole book. Spend all your lottery winnings. Take a weekend trip. Learn how to swim. Or cook. Or dance salsa. You can travel to the Moon.

Marty, the former pill-popper who'd sadly lost his daughter, graduated on a

Thursday. He'd cried during the ceremony, but I couldn't tell if they were tears of joy or hopelessness.

After he left rehab, Marty was like Schrödinger's cat to me. Until Sunday. That's when we got the sad news that he'd ODed, three days after graduating. The cat in the box was dead.

Most people never take their own addictions seriously until they watch someone close to them self-destruct. The devastating news, while sobering, made a lot of us want to lean on the crutches we'd become so used to, so reliant on. And if we were surrounded by enablers, we probably would have. But with some willpower and a little encouragement, we channeled that raw emotion through art— my favorite outlet.

"What did you paint today?" I was never sure if the priest's interest in my work was genuine. If not, he sure did a good job faking it.

"One of the nurses here put on an episode of Bob Ross and we were supposed to paint a meadow scene with *happy little trees*. They asked me nicely not to paint another portrait of Marty."

"So you obliged?" the priest asked.

"I painted the meadow and hid Marty's face in the water."

"Aida, if you're that talented of an

artist, why don't you go to art school when you're feeling better?"

"'Feeling better'?"

"Okay, poor choice of words. I apologize—you know what I meant."

"I feel great," I was a bit on edge.

"When you get out, I just think art school is something you should consider. That's all."

"When I get out? Now you're the one making this sound like prison."

As the priest spoke and continued to dig himself into a deeper hole, I tried to take a step back—a method I'd learned from Dr. Monterro, not necessarily for recovery but just for interpersonal communication. I realized I'd been neglecting any struggles the priest might've been dealing with and projecting my anger onto him.

"What's wrong?" I interrupted. "Tell me about it."

Sometimes it was fun to play the therapist instead of the patient. It's almost freeing, in a way, to learn about somebody else's problems—makes you feel better about your own. No matter how together a person's shit seems, he's got tons of things going on in his life and even more in his head. You don't know what he's been through.

Had the priest found a way to teach

me lessons without making me hate him?
I never liked being talked down to or
treated like a lesser person. Maybe I was
taking comfort in the fact that his problems seemed too genuine to just be for
show.

JUNIOR YEAR of high school, the
twins got suspended for cursing at a sub-
stitute teacher. Well, Beth got suspended.
David wasn't even in the class, but he refused to go to school on principle. It was
his form of protest, since it'd been the
same sub who had written him up months
earlier for sleeping in class. He claimed
the woman had a vendetta against his
family.

During the week they were out, Mark
and I stopped by their house every day
after school. They kept trying to convince
us to join the movement and boycott
school with them. I played hooky one day,
but Mark made sure I went in the next
day because the twins were the type who'd
take people down with them, according to
Mark. I wasn't sure what he'd meant by
that at the time, but after coming across
so many different kinds of people in rehab, I'd become pretty familiar with the
type.

Mark was funny in this way: He'd
complain and have all of these critical

things to say about the twins' behavior,
but he'd never leave them hanging. Maybe
he was a good person, or maybe he got off
seeing other people spiral—either way, he
was always there. Which is why I was so
confused when he suddenly wasn't there
for me. As I made friends with people in
the center, I wondered if my relationships
lacked substance because I preferred it
that way, or because my tendency to use
people was so see-through that they
wanted nothing to do with me.

"Why don't I have any friends?"

"What are you talking about, Aida?"

"Nobody so much as texted me after
my mom died. Not one of my friends."

"See, you just said you have friends."

"Not in the mood for jokes, Father." I
thought about Mark and the twins a lot in
rehab. Was I one of those people who
brought others down with them? Did the
priest see me that way?

"Hey, how do you see me?"

"How do I see you? What does that
mean?"

"It means—"

"I'm just not sure what you want me
to say here, Aida. I see you as a person."

Somehow, that was the most musical
thing he could've said. 'A person.' That's
what I was to him. Not a person recovering from drug addiction. Not a person

112

overcoming the loss of her mother. Not a person dealing with a heap of internal and external struggles. And not *just another* person. But a person.

"I see you as a person who is kind-hearted and has a unique, though sometimes wicked, sense of humor. And you—"

"Father, I wasn't looking for any specific answer. I just wanted to know if my behavior could be seen as—"

"Selfish."

"Yeah, selfish. How did you know what I was gonna say?"

"Maybe it's time to stop assuming we're so different."

10

BELONGING

*For I know the plans I have for you, declares the Lord,
plans for welfare and not for evil, to give you a future
and a hope.*
Jeremiah 29:11

I PICKED Aida up from the treatment center on a Friday. I had the car wait outside as we signed her out and grabbed her belongings. She'd packed pretty lightly for a young woman—she wasn't into the latest fashion trends, and she hardly wore makeup. She didn't need it, really. I could tell her skin had gotten clearer while she was at the facility, probably a result of eating healthier. Lord knows what her diet had been like in the weeks preceding.

As we made our way toward the doors, we heard a man's voice call from behind us. "Best of luck, Aida!"

We both turned around, she faster than I, to see a man in a white coat with a big smile on his face. Aida responded to him with a nod, a chuckle, and a wave.

"Who was that?" I asked, opening the front doors of the facility.

"Oh, just one of the doctors I worked with. Doctor Monterro."

"That's Dr. Monterro? No wonder you always sounded so excited when you mentioned his name on the phone."

"What's that supposed to mean?"

"Nothing's wrong with having a little crush, Aida."

She smiled. "He's nice. And a lot of what he said helped me."

"Uh huh..."

"...He's not bad to look at, either."

We shared a laugh. Then Aida took a deep breath and turned toward me. "Can we walk back to the church? It's gorgeous out."

I looked at her, surprised. "The church? Don't you want to go home?"

"Eventually, yeah. But there's nothing for me there."

"Aida, the church is at least a twelve-mile walk..."

"So, what's the rush?" she said, as she began rolling her lone suitcase down the sidewalk. After apologizing to the driver, I told him we wouldn't need a ride back to the other end of the city. He pulled away, reluctantly, and shook his head as he examined us in his rearview mirror: two aimless pairs of legs, just tracing our paths down one tree-lined street on a vast sphere full of fellow wanderers, aimless all the same.

We made it about three and a half miles before Aida got tired. Or hungry. I don't remember which it was—I was tired after three and a half blocks. Surprisingly, we didn't say much during our walk. It was nice, actually: enjoying the weather, the sounds, the sights. She led us into a hoagie shop, and I treated her to lunch.

You can learn a lot about a person from his or her sandwich order. For example, people who like to try new things will go with the most exotic-sounding item on the menu. More conventional sandwich eaters stick to the classics, with no surprises. It's not that these people are closed-minded—they are just hesitant when it comes to change.

After placing our orders, we sat down to wait for our food. Aida picked a table by the window. "I like to people-watch," she said. I told her I had no problem with observing, as long as she wasn't judging people solely based on appearance. "People-watching and watching people are two totally different things," she clarified.

Aida was funny. I didn't remember her making too many jokes over the phone. Then again, she'd been in rehabilitation and mourning.

"How many Jethro Tull records do you think this guy owns?" I said, subtly pointing to a heavily bearded, vest-wearing passerby on the street. I wanted to play along with her people-watching game.

"What's Jet Rotull?" Aida replied. "And hey, now you're the one judging people by the way they look!"

Our hoagies arrived just as she'd caught me being a hypocrite, something priests were certainly not supposed to get caught doing. But I'm human—it wasn't the first time I hadn't practiced what I'd preached, and I was sure it wouldn't be the last.

The sandwiches looked delicious. After all, we'd worked up quite the appetite on our walk over. I peered down at Aida's meal.

"Oh, that looks good. What'd you get again?"

"A pesto chicken hoagie with mozz and sundried tomatoes," she said, taking a bite. "How about you?"

"Me? I haven't had one in a while, so I went with a turkey club."

THAT WEEKEND, I invited Aida to join some of our parishioners for St. Anthony's monthly Sunday breakfast. I thought it'd be good for her—I could introduce her around, so she'd be acquainted with more than just me. Some of our community was quite conservative in nature, but others were extremely open-minded. There was a decent balance, especially at church-sponsored events, but I wasn't sure how the more traditional bunch would respond to Aida's sudden active involvement in the community.

Most people who attended our recovery programs and support groups didn't normally participate in community functions, so these factions of people rarely overlapped. For people like Evan, it wasn't uncommon to attend Mass and gravitate toward the back. The 'holiest' churchgoers usually sat toward the front, so they were none the wiser.

These people already knew about Aida, though—from her drug use to her estranged father to her promiscuous mother. It pained me to even think that word about a woman I never had the pleasure of meeting, but that's how information spread through the church community: gossip.

Somebody spoke to someone who knew another person's cousin, who knew Aida's mother. An absurd, wretched game of telephone, but that was reality. And like wildfire, every attendant of Sunday breakfast had caught wind of a young girl who had nearly overdosed getting another chance at a virtuous life, coming to one of our church events.

Aida arrived wearing what I'd assumed was the nicest casual dress she owned: navy blue with a floral pattern, and a skirt that flowed down to about knee-length. She wore a faded red cardigan over it, to match the bright red floral print on her dress. Her clothes were fine, but she seemed so out of place. When she walked in, everyone stopped dead in their tracks. I rushed over to welcome her.

I could tell people were judging. I stood in front of every individual in that room at least once a week, so I knew what faces they made when encountering someone or something unfamiliar. They were unamused by the unknown. New frightened them, and I noticed a majority of my most loyal parishioners directing the same look they gave strangers at Mass toward Aida.

"Glad you could make it!" I gave Aida

a hug as a physical, no-questions-asked display to onlookers. She was welcome at St. Anthony's.

"Me too," she responded. Her eyes wandered around the room, as others darted their gazes so not to intersect. "Cool party."

Aida ambled toward the table where I'd organized the breakfast spread, complete with bagels, fruit, coffee, and juice. When her back was to the crowd, she became the main attraction. But with every slight turn of her head, they diverted their attention to each other, to their phones, or to wherever was convenient. She opted for a garlic bagel with cream cheese and a cup of orange juice. Before I could comment, she reached for a banana.

"Don't worry, Father, I made sure to grab some fruit."

"Am I that predictable?" I joked.

"I'd call it consistent."

I let Aida enjoy her breakfast and went to exchange pleasantries with some of our other members. As I spoke to the Zoe Roberson—a woman in her late thirties, originally from Seattle—I smiled at Aida from across the sea of people. She smiled back, conversing with a small group of new mothers. The babies seemed to love her red cardigan.

"Mrs. Roberson, where are Tom and

Jacob this morning?" I asked. "I don't remember seeing them at Mass."

"Oh, Tom had to run Jake to his soccer game," she said, smiling with her mouth closed. "We're so sorry, Father. Can't miss the playoffs!"

Her response sounded rehearsed, as if she were hoping I wouldn't ask that question but had a strong feeling I would. I felt bad for being predictable again.

"No, no, I'm glad Jacob went to his game. He loves playing, doesn't he?"

"Yes he does," Zoe agreed. "But what about Mass?"

"There's going to come a day when Jacob is my age and can't play soccer anymore. But God," I said, "God will always be there for him. Even when soccer's not." She nodded and laughed, this time smiling in a way that didn't feel forced. "Might as well enjoy it now!" I added.

AS I started to clean up, several parishioners offered to help—some just to be nice, but some for real. I declined their offers, as this was my way of showing gratitude for their loyalty and active participation. Aida had been long gone when Ms. Carol Waters stopped beside me to whisper something cryptic in my ear, with her soft-spoken voice and heavy southern accent.

"She's nice, the girl. But I hope you see through her like we do."

The elderly Ms. Waters left before I could process what she'd said. She had to have meant Aida, I assumed. See through what, though? What did Carol think she knew about Aida that I didn't already know? And who was *we*?

Immediately, I thought back to when I'd passed by Carol and a group of older adults during the breakfast. Out of context, what I overheard meant nothing to me. But with her unprovoked pseudo-threat still ringing in my ear, the phrases 'poor influence' and 'I hope he's thinking of the children' suddenly took shape into a cohesive message.

Ms. Waters was the last to exit the church annex, leaving behind her a wake of uncertainty. I questioned the faith I'd put in Aida and her recovery—and as unfounded as that doubt was, it was the first time I'd even stopped to think: Who was this mysterious girl I'd allowed into my life? Was I right to welcome her into our community so swiftly? Why hadn't I asked myself these questions earlier?

Truth was, I felt drawn to Aida for some reason. It was nothing physical or emotional, but spiritual rather. Something about this troubled young woman resonated with me deeply—perhaps on a deeper level than I'd connected with Evan. I couldn't help but believe there was a higher power at work, behind the scenes, that had placed us in the same alley of the same city on the same night. Unbeknownst to Aida, our roles could've easily been switched that night—me unconscious, empty bottle at my side, she reluctantly springing to my aid.

Section Three:
Fall, Part 2

————————

11

INTERVENTION

I MUST'VE caught a stomach bug from one of those germy kids at the church breakfast. Everyone I talked to was nice and all, but I didn't see myself becoming friends with a bunch of people I had nothing in common with. Regardless of how welcome the priest made it clear I was, I still considered myself an outsider.

Not sure how long that feeling would last, I kind of ghosted the priest for about a week. I'd even skipped the church's addiction recovery support group meeting thing. I knew showing up at one event and then disappearing wouldn't help my cause, but I really felt like shit. I mean, I had the priest's cellphone number, but I didn't feel like calling him—especially not just to exaggerate my illness for some sort of sympathy.

I didn't want sympathy. I didn't want someone to bring me soup. I didn't even want my mom back to take care of me. All I wanted was to fit in, to belong somewhere. And at that moment, St. Anthony's was my best chance to have some semblance of a normal, social, functional life. The church was my opportunity to regain that humanity I'd numbed myself from feeling—that personal connection to another individual that made getting up in the morning worth it.

Part of my problem was that I wasn't having an easy time adapting to so many new things at once. My mom was gone, and I'd made sure my drugs were gone as well. But just because I wasn't letting myself get high anymore didn't mean I was suddenly okay with who I was. No, you don't fix insecurity that fast. It was now my responsibility to rebuild my self-worth, using the foundation my treatment had helped me lay down. At least, that's what Dr. Monterro had told me.

The week dragged on, and my nausea didn't seem to go away. Sunday morning rolled around and I woke up to vomit for the fifth time in seven days. I'd been planning on heading to Mass at 8:30 a.m., but clearly that wasn't going to happen.

After a refreshing hot shower, I stood in the bathroom with my phone in my hand. It was 9:14—too early to call the priest because Mass was still going on. Walking into my bedroom, I placed my phone on the nightstand. As I threw some sweats on, I stared at the phone, waiting for it to jump toward me and force me to call him. He had to have known I was okay, right? Otherwise, he would've called me by then, or stopped by if he was truly concerned.

If he'd been genuinely worried that I had gone on a bender and snorted my way into a coma, I assumed he would've checked up on me. What, had he investigated every alley in Philadelphia? Did he pass by my place to make sure the lights were on and there were signs of life?

My phone lit up. It was a text from my friend Mark. Though, I don't know how good of a friend I'd consider him, since this was the first time he'd contacted me since my mom died. Sadly, he was my only sober-ish friend, and probably the best one I had.

Heard ur mom died and u went to rehab?? U ok?

I told him that, surprisingly, I was doing fine. Then I sarcastically told him I must've missed him at my mom's wake and funeral.

128

Aida, I'm super sorry!!! I had no idea. The twins don't tell me anything. I don't even talk to those ppl anymore. Are u alone now?

I wanted to tell him I was always alone, but I deleted it after typing it out because it sounded too emo. My phone read 10:03 a.m.—the perfect time to call the priest between the morning and early afternoon Masses.

I'm coming over. Don't go anywhere, I'll be right there.

As much as I missed Mark—and any kind of friendship, for that matter—I was in no condition to host a guest.

Actually, can we take a rain check? I answered. *I've been pretty sick for the past week, throwing up every morning.*

Yeah, absolutely, he texted back. *Just let me know when ur free.*

I thanked him for texting me, even if it had been over a month since we'd last spoken.

U got it, A. Haha feel better. U probably either got the flu or ur preggers!

THREE DAYS. That's the normal amount of time sperm can live in a woman's body, according to Google. In ideal conditions—ideal for whom, I'm not sure—that number can get up to five days. I hadn't had sex in over a month. Shit, I'd been in rehab for like four weeks.

Can you get pregnant from a sex dream? I'd thought about Dr. Monterro a few times, but I didn't think that was possible. Maybe I'd sat on a toilet seat that was compromised while at the treatment center? If I recalled correctly back to high school health class, I was much more likely to contract a venereal disease from a toilet seat than I was a baby. Not sure which would've been worse in this case.

If my mom were alive, I knew exactly how she would've reacted: "Well, I'm surprised it didn't happen sooner." And she would've been right, too. Before my recent attempt to transform myself, I was extremely lackadaisical about choosing when, where, and who to fuck. And I was never careful. So, this scare happening just as I was beginning to piece together the broken shards of my life was... ironic.

I threw down my phone so I'd stop Googling stuff. Maybe I was overreacting. My period was like nine days late, but I chalked that up to the tremendous stress I'd undergone—an amalgamation of my mom's death, withdrawal, the rehab process itself, adjusting to my new life, and finally being sober enough to realize I didn't like who I was on or off drugs.

I didn't know for sure that I was pregnant, and wouldn't have an actual answer until I took one of those tests I had to pee on. But wouldn't venturing out to the pharmacy to buy the test be admitting defeat?

Another half hour passed, with me still lying in bed, contemplating my next move. I didn't want to be in limbo anymore. The ambiguity was freaking me out. Determined, I slipped some socks and sneakers on, swung on a coat, and walked briskly to the pharmacy around the corner. Hood up, head down—a woman on a mission.

When I got home, I ripped open the four packages I'd purchased. I tried the first one, following the instructions closely as I held it under my nervous, erratic stream of piss.

THE CATHOLIC Church believes that Mary, the 'Blessed Virgin,' was born without sin—that God himself preserved her from the time she'd been conceived, hence an 'immaculate conception.'

I was certainly not without sin, and even with my newfound sobriety and abstinence, my body of work was far from sainthood. I'd only been religious again for like six weeks, but I couldn't resist drawing parallels.

Mary had an angel come down to her to announce that she'd been chosen as the mother of God's only son. I had no such encounter—no angel, no warning. Unless I did and I'd just been too high to notice or remember. But the connection was inescapable: No man, no sex, yet somehow with child.

What was I going to do? Fuck thinking nine months ahead. What about nine hours, or minutes? Who would I tell first? Should I maintain that I didn't sleep with anybody to warrant this predicament? Who the hell would believe me?

I pictured my story eventually turning into some round-the-clock news saga, something to fill the media's gaps during a slow week. The country divided: half doubting my celibacy, the other half willing to entertain the idea of a supernatural occurrence. Conspiracy theorists pointing toward alien abduction as the potential explanation, and a weekly podcast to go along with it. Hot takes from all the talking heads on TV and radio, just trying to get their two cents in, as if it would matter. Churches from all around the world rushing to condemn or embrace me.

Which side of the aisle would my new church be on? The people I'd met at St. Anthony's were mostly nice, but I could sense an air of phoniness. There were some churchgoers at the breakfast who wouldn't speak to me or make extended eye contact—they'd just shoot hostile glances in my direction every so often.

And most importantly, what would the priest believe?

It would've been at least seven or eight weeks before I could get a paternity test, probably twelve or thirteen to be safe. But I might already be showing twelve weeks down the road. And how would a paternity test have helped anyway? I didn't have the slightest clue as to who the father might have been. Normally, that happens because a woman sleeps with too many dudes, but this was the exact opposite problem. There were no dudes; I hadn't fucked anyone recently.

Who was I kidding? I didn't want to think nine months or twelve weeks ahead because I wanted to take care of the situation long before then. I felt guilty for it, and I had no one to talk to about it. I wrestled with my thoughts, but I was no match for them. After two sleepless nights, I felt compelled to take action—the only type of action I saw fit.

THE CLINIC looked just like any other building. I made sure I got there early enough to steer clear of the wave of protesters that gathered outside in the middle of the day. As I walked toward the entrance, I stopped my arm from reaching out to open the door. This wasn't me. I wasn't going to get rid of this baby without so much as talking to someone—maybe the priest?—about it first. So, I retreated back home to figure shit out.

I'd been avoiding the man who saved me because I didn't want him to see me differently. He'd put so much time and effort into helping me reassemble the puzzle that was my life, or at least organize the pieces into a pile that resembled a person who was trying. Disappointing the priest was one of my biggest fears. Unfortunately, my fear of having to care for another living thing far outweighed any potential disappointment. Fuck it. This was something I had to do.

The next day, I ventured back down to Planned Parenthood, more determined than my previous trip. This time, I didn't attempt to walk in right away. I sat on a bench across the street and just stared at the front door for nearly two hours. Time moved around me, but my focus never broke. It was like as soon as I got close to the place, doubts would start swirling around in my head. And the longer my ass pressed against that cold, metal bench, the less likely it was that I would get up and follow through with what I'd promised myself I'd do before I left home.

I went back the next day, sitting on

that same bench in the pouring rain. Each drop burned like acid on my skin—a pain that almost seemed purifying. After about an hour and a half or so, a young woman opened the door of the health center and stepped out into the rain, looking both ways before she darted across the street. She came right for me, umbrella in hand.

"We've seen you out here for the past few days," she said, sitting next to me on the wet bench. I stayed silent, the rain's moisture making the cold metal sting through my leggings. "You know, it's a lot drier and warmer inside. Would you like to go talk in there? I promise, we don't bite." She giggled.

I took a deep breath and nodded, turning toward her to finally make eye contact.

"Good. Okay, then," she said as she stood up, holding the umbrella to shield both of our heads. I got up from the bench, shivering. The woman grabbed me by the arm, gently, and began to guide me across the street. "My name's Dorothy, by the way."

"It's my twenty-first birthday today," I said, nodding to myself.

"Well, happy birthday then. Let's get you inside."

12

QUESTIONS OF FAITH

Anyone who takes the life of a human being is to be put to death.
Leviticus 24:17

MY FATHER didn't raise me to be the worrying type. But following the community breakfast, it was as if Aida had dropped off the face of the earth, and I was concerned. She didn't attend any meetings at the church, nor did she join us for any services. The two-week period of not hearing from her was the most attached I'd ever been to my cell phone, checking it frantically after every Mass and meeting, and pulling it out of my pocket whenever I felt something that resembled a vibration.

I prayed that Aida hadn't relapsed, and I desperately hoped she was okay. But I knew the process of adapting to a new life was something she had to conquer on her own. Of course, I'd be there to help her along the way, but ultimately she'd need to not only prove to herself that she could do it—she needed to prove that she wanted to.

I contemplated riding the bus to her side of town a few times, just to make sure she wasn't in trouble. My faith, however, prevented me from checking up on her— my faith in Aida, my faith in God, and my faith in the human condition. Growth was a major part of this condition, and I had spent entire nights staring at the dark ceiling, convincing myself that Aida recognized the magnitude any small decision could have on the rest of her life.

With Carol's whispered message still echoing in my ear, I had my doubts about Aida. But I wasn't going to let it shape my opinion of the person in whom I'd already invested so much. One Sunday after Mass, Carol approached me again.

"Phenomenal homily, Father," she said. "What a wonderful message today."

"I appreciate it, Ms. Waters. I hope those who needed to hear it were listening, too."

"Speaking of which..." I already knew where this was headed. "...What ever happened to that young girl, the one you brought to our breakfast last month?"

"First of all, I didn't 'bring' her—she was invited, and she came." I lost my composure a bit. "She's as much a part of our community as you and I are. And second, her name is Aida."

"Excuse me if I struck a chord, Father, but she ain't much a member of our community if she doesn't show up to Mass."

"Sorry, no, you're right," I instinctively backtracked. "She's just going through a tough time is all."

"Maybe it's for the better, then," Ms. Waters said, as she offered a closed-mouth smile, nodded, and walked away.

AIDA CALLED me on a Wednesday morning, asking if we could meet that afternoon by the fountain at Logan Square. I was thrilled to hear her voice, but I sensed she had something on her mind that she was too afraid or nervous to communicate over the phone.

I arrived about twenty minutes or so before she did. I didn't mind waiting, though—it was a clear day, with blue skies and the faded green grass framing a medley of autumn hues. Slight breeze at my

138

back, I enjoyed a steamy oolong tea from a family-owned café in Sister Cities Park. Whatever Aida had to say, I was certain I was more afraid and nervous to hear it than she was to talk about it.

She stepped into my line of vision slowly and unconfidently, almost as if she'd been tiptoeing. As I noticed her from a distance, I gave her a friendly wave—after all, we'd gone from speaking quite frequently to complete radio silence. Aida didn't wave back. Instead, she continued walking toward me, with her head down and sunglasses covering her eyes.

"Aida, it's great to see you," I broke the ice.

"Father... I'm sorry. I don't know where to start."

"Just talk to me. This isn't confession," I assured her, wanting her to feel safe. We'd had so many honest and open discussions, and I hoped this conversation would be no different. "What happened? Is everything okay?"

She removed her wayfarers and tried to conceal her tears. The face I saw was not that of the empowered, new-lease-on-life Aida I remembered. She looked defeated, as if the stress of her mother's death, her addiction, and her identity crisis caught up to her all at once. I placed my hand on her shoulder, anticipating her to flinch.

"I'm pregnant," she mumbled as she allowed her head to fall into my chest.

Unsure how to react, I held her but didn't respond—half-hoping she'd take my silence as an invitation to expand on her bombshell, half-hoping my ears had deceived me.

"But it's not mine," she continued.

After a pause, I responded, "What does that mean, Aida?"

She giggled. "Nobody's going to believe me," she said deliriously. "Not even you."

"If you're pregnant and the baby isn't yours... then whose is it?"

"Before Mary got pregnant, God sent the angel Gabriel to announce that He'd chosen her to bring His only Son into this world."

Now I laughed. "I see you've been doing some reading." But then I noticed the sincerity on her face. The absence of glow. The lack of smirk or side-eye that made Aida *Aida*. "Hey..."

"I know I'm not a virgin—far from it, actually. But that doesn't mean—"

I cut her off. "Aida, how do you know you're pregnant?"

She broke eye contact and took a deep breath before reaching into her bag. As she pulled out a sealed clear plastic bag, she exhaled.

"I took four pregnancy tests and they all say the same thing."

"Have you been carrying those around with you, or did you just bring them to prove something to me?"

"I keep them because, sometimes, I think the past few weeks have been a cruel nightmare. And these remind me that it's fucking real."

"What makes it a nightmare?"

"I went to the clinic last week, with the intention of getting an abortion." I tried my hardest not to let my facial expressions make her feel judged. I wasn't judging her. But real-time reactions, though visceral, can give the wrong impression. "It took me three separate trips to go inside," she continued. "Three times. And the only reason I went in the last time was because it was pouring and one of the women who worked there was nice enough to come outside and talk to me."

Again, I was speechless. I motioned my hand as if to prompt her.

"I couldn't go through with it—not because I don't believe in abortion or think it's wrong. But because, as soon as I walked in the door and shook off some of the rain, I felt violently sick. I immediately vomited all over the floor and bolted out, crying. Like, I've been nervous-sick

before, and this was not that. This was...
something else."

"A sign?" I suggested.

"Maybe."

"From God?"

"Father, I didn't come here to talk
about my feelings. Do you believe me or
not?"

"Aida, and I don't mean anything
negative by this, but what makes you
think God would send Jesus down here
again? And there are three and a half–
billion women in the world—why would
He choose you to help Him?"

"Why not me?"

AIDA'S   CONFESSION—though   I
hated to consider it that—was a lot to take
in. To avoid making any snap judgments,
I looked at it objectively: Her mother
passes away, and she resorts to substances because she thinks they're her
crutch. Then, she gets a second chance
and takes advantage of it, completing her
entire recovery program without a hiccup.
After disappearing for two weeks, she
wants to meet me somewhere, instead of
coming to the church. Then, of course, she
tells me she's pregnant—and believes it's
an act of God.

That two-week span seemed to be the
missing puzzle piece. I wasn't ready to

chastise Aida based on my unfounded assumptions. I also wasn't ready to support her and take her word for it. I needed something more, some kind of proof that her pregnancy was truly God's work and not her own doing.

I realized my hypocrisy. I so often preached about how believing something involves faith, and doesn't always require evidence. When we actually believe something to be true, it means not needing proof of any kind.

As a man of faith, I turned to God. I prayed that He'd show me a small sign that I could trust Aida's word. At the park, she'd mentioned her experience at the medical clinic. She considered it a sign, but what was it a sign of? Was God trying to tell her that abortion would've been the wrong course of action? Or was He communicating something deeper?

"God, I'm struggling to understand your message here." I knelt down beside my bed and placed my elbows on the mattress. "I've tried to see all angles of Evan's unfortunate fate, and I still haven't been able to—but I accept his story's ending because it was a complete arc. I watched him transform using sheer willpower. But with Aida, there's no closure. She's starting from scratch, much like Evan had done. Except she has fewer resources, less

support, less willpower. She has less like-
lihood of a happy ending, and a virtual
certainty of relapse. That is, if she hasn't
fallen back into old habits already."

My conversations with God didn't
normally take this tone. But I was frustrated.

"And Evan didn't even get a happy
ending. What about his family? What
about his brother he'd just reconnected
with? His nieces and nephew? He was a
good man." I stopped and looked around
my room, my eyes fixated on the crucifix
hanging on my wall. I laughed to myself,
"Listen to me, I'm letting myself get
worked up talking to someone who isn't
even there."

My praying had devolved into a
Seinfeld-esque airing of grievances toward God. "And do you know how I know
you're not there? Because you let Evan
die, after all he did for his country, his
family, and himself. And now, you've
made a young girl's life—which was troubled to begin with—spiral out of control
just as she was getting it back on track.
Or, you've placed your Son's life in the
hands of an unreliable drug addict."

As the words left my mouth, I wondered if I'd felt this way all along. It was
certainly freeing to say them out loud—
because I knew I meant every single one.

Since I considered myself responsible for seeing her recovery through, I was upset with Aida and disappointed with myself. I felt as if I'd betrayed her by not checking in during her two-week hiatus, and that God had betrayed me.

"Which is it, God? Are you essentially ruining Aida's life and her child's?" I screamed in no particular direction, while pointing at my crucifix. "Or are you entrusting the same girl I found half-dead in an alley to raise the Second Coming of the Savior on whom a third of the world bases its belief system?"

Clearly, praying was done. I sat on my bed and continued venting, both about and to God. "She's not virtuous enough. She's a wild card. What, do you have something to prove? Mary was born without sin and had Joseph, her soon-to-be husband, to help her. Aida has one man in her life, that I know of: me."

I WANTED to be there for Aida. I truly did. But I couldn't get past the feeling that I was being intentionally deceived. I'd spent a lot of time with hundreds of people who were trying to improve every day. They were taking steps forward, and putting faith first—using God as their fuel to get better. I also considered myself one of those people.

If Aida were right—if she had by some miracle become the vehicle for the Lord's ultimate message—then God would be doing a remarkable disservice to all of His loyal worshippers. How could He put that type of responsibility on her shoulders? With all of the decent people out there trying, why would He choose to intervene in the life of somebody who wouldn't even be alive if it weren't for me?

There was nobody else to talk to about the situation. I'd reached my limit on yelling at God, so I invited Aida to the church for a private conversation. This time, I wanted a confession. I needed the truth.

She showed up a little late but appeared happier than our last encounter. Surprisingly, she entered the confessional upon my request—with no hesitation nor dispute.

"Good morning, Father," she began. "It's been... a really long time since my last confession."

"Good morning, Aida. You can say whatever you want in here, as long as it's the truth."

"Well, I have a few questions first."

"Fire away."

"If you do believe me... Who do we tell? I don't want to be an overnight celebrity or featured on an episode of *I Don't*

146

Know How I Got Pregnant. I'm not sure
that's even a show, but it could be and I
want no part of it."

"Why do we have to tell anyone? I'm
not certain it's something that needs to be
advertised."

"I want to be involved in this church's
community, Father," she said, her eyes
burning holes through the divider. "And I
know a bunch of people already look at
me with disdain. How do you think they'll
respond to an outrageous claim like this?
Or would I rather them just think I got
knocked up by a stranger?"

I understood her concern, and unfortunately, I'd previously been so caught up
in how this situation affected me and other churchgoers, that I didn't even stop to
think about the immediate fallout from
Aida's perspective.

"And I was thinking," said Aida.
"What if me throwing up at Planned
Parenthood wasn't God's way of saying
abortion was wrong? What if it was a sign
that I need to have this specific baby?"

"Wha—what are you talking about?" I
opened the screen that divided us.

"Like, maybe God is making it known
that this particular child is important."

"Aida, every child is important."

"But what if this one is—"

"The Second Coming."

"Exactly! Not everybody starts vomiting uncontrollably when they try to get an abortion. Maybe this kid is special."

"Maybe you didn't really want to go through with it."

"Oh, and I want a baby?"

"What do you want me to say?"

"That you don't think I'm lying. That you'll be there, because nobody else is."

What if she was hiding something? What if she'd made a mistake and fallen back into her old ways? What if she made the whole thing up to cover a relapse? I didn't know how to react in the moment.

Or worse yet: What if she was telling the truth?

13

CRUCIFIXION

THE PRIEST believed me. I think. At least, he was trying to. He was too nice to say he didn't, and he was too righteous to say he'd have to wait to see a paternity test. "Seeing isn't believing," he said. Also, had God put the baby inside of me, he was worried the child's DNA would've left doctors scratching their heads. So, it wouldn't have been a good idea to go tell everyone about it.

For the priest to look me in the eyes, tell me he bought my story, and agree to provide moral support throughout the pregnancy, I had to swear to him that I hadn't had sex with anyone since before rehab. It was also the only way he'd invite me back to church events. I knew that I didn't technically need to be invited to any community get-togethers, but I felt out of place if nobody wanted me there. If I was going to be a part of the community, I needed to make friends as soon as possible—because things would get infinitely more complicated once I was sporting a baby bump. So, having the priest on my side was a good start.

These church people already had their cliques. Who was going to want to make friends with the much-gossiped recovered druggie who'd suddenly shown up pregnant? Rumors would have been one thing, but these weren't just rumors—it was all completely real. And someone in the St. Anthony's inner circle was bound to have seen me at one of those NA meetings, or at least to have known someone who'd met me.

Being an outcast was the last thing I wanted. I'd been an outcast for most of my teenage years. But when I got home from school, my mom would always be there. Now, without her around, I didn't know what made me feel more alone: being at home or being out in the world. At least home was familiar to me. Out there was foreign.

Life is so much easier when you're numb, when you don't allow yourself to feel things. Emotions cloud up your judgment. They drive you to act in an un-reasonable way, and the biggest issue is that your feelings make it seem reasona-ble. Feelings cause unnecessary stress.

What will others think of me? Will they like me? What if they don't? Many of us base our entire identities on who oth-ers see us to be. That's why I'd preferred closing myself off to the world. Everyone outside my bubble was just an extra—a nameless, faceless, inconsequential body that existed simply to take up space and make my life seem less empty.

But my life *was* empty. That's what being sober made me realize. The whole time, I'd been an extra in my own life, meandering through scenes and phoning it in instead of confidently being myself and putting together a story with sub-stance. A story worth telling, a life worth living.

The priest had me believing I could do exactly that. I didn't know where I'd be without his support. I just hoped he'd continue to have my back while I assimi-lated into the church community.

A WOMAN named Zoe introduced herself to me after Sunday morning mass. She was gorgeous: piercing blue eyes, an adorable blonde bob, barely any wrinkles. I could tell her hair was natural from her blonde eyebrows. She was impressively attractive for a mom—and a religious one, at that.

When I was younger, my dad always used to joke that you could never find beautiful women in church. He'd say, "Pretty women got nothing to pray about. They already have everything they need." Mom, of course, would nudge him to remind him that she went to church, and then he'd scrunch up his face like he was thinking about it. Without fail, he'd reply, "I said what I said."

Zoe was the nicest, realest person I'd met at the church up to that point. Her whole family was sweet. Her husband Tom was a total D.I.L.F., and their son Jacob was fairly tolerable for a nine-year-old. Maybe kids weren't so bad.

"Don't get the wrong impression," Zoe said. "He's well-behaved in public—especially in church—but once we get home, he'll go back to being an animal." She giggled.

Without that half-laugh at the end, I wouldn't have known she was joking. Was she?

"He seems like a good kid, though," I said, almost sticking up for Jacob.

"Oh, he's great," she admitted. "Our Jacob is more than anything my husband and I could've hoped for." Zoe leaned in toward me, to whisper: "And he wasn't even planned."

As she pulled away from my ear, I noticed a fresh sense of relief on her face, as if she'd been waiting to tell someone that minor fact. She looked brighter, her eyes somehow reflecting light more honestly. "Sorry, I've never said that within these walls." I nodded. "Truth is, Tom and I wanted to travel, you know? But I got pregnant, and I don't know... Things work out, I guess."

"I feel like that's pretty common nowadays, though. A lot of kids aren't planned. Is it that big of a deal?" I may have already known the answer to my question before I asked it.

"Well, obviously I wouldn't want my son to feel unwanted," she responded. "But the people here, they judge you for anything and everything. They consider whatever's unfamiliar uncouth."

"Trust me, I completely understand that. I was getting such weird looks at the last breakfast."

"I thought I remembered seeing you there! People probably looked at you that way because all they knew about you was... well, you know."

I didn't know. The drugs? My runaway father? My dead mom? What had the priest told these people about me?

"Sorry," Zoe said. "People talk, and it's tough to tune out the gossip."

It was high school all over again.

NO MATTER how much I tried not to let it get to me, I hated that people—strangers, no less—were talking about me behind my back. They didn't know me, and didn't even have the decency to give me a chance before branding me as the impure drug addict with a troubled past. To find out exactly what was being said about me, I put on my friendliest face and began poking around amongst my fellow churchgoers.

"Hi! I don't believe we've met," I introduced myself to a group of elderly women. "My name's Aida. I'm new to the church."

"Oh, well good morning, Aida," said one of the women.

"Welcome!" said another.

"I'm Carol."

"Jodie."

"And I'm Susan."

"Great to meet all of you," I said, trying to match their fakeness. "How long have you been coming to St. Anthony's?"

Jodie answered first. "I've been living in the city for, say, 25 years now. So, about that long."

"I've been coming here my whole

life," followed Susan.

"And you?" I prompted Carol.

"Me? My husband and I moved here from West Virginia about twelve years ago." I could tell from her drawl. "What brings you to St. Anthony's... Aida, was it?"

"Yes. My family used to go to Immaculate when I was younger, but a lot of things changed, and my path eventually led me here."

"Everything happens for a reason, sweetie," said Susan.

"Good morning, folks!" The priest projected from outside the doorway, approaching us. "Everything all right over here?"

"Of course," Carol assured. "The girls and I were just heading to brunch. Goodbye, Aida." She didn't sound like she wanted to cross paths again.

"I'll see you around," I countered. As the ladies walked away, the priest pulled me aside.

"What are you doing, Aida?"

"Making friends."

"But why them?"

"How much have you told your friends about me?" I was on the verge of tears—after all, my hormones were pretty out of whack.

"Aida, they're not all my friends.

Some are friendly, but most are just people who go to my church."

"You didn't answer my question. Clearly some of these people know what I was going through. Their donations helped pay for my treatment. What else do they know?"

The priest broke eye contact and motioned for me to follow him to a room with a little more privacy than the main entrance of the church. He took me into an empty classroom-looking space and unfolded two of the chairs leaned up against the wall. After offering me one, he sat down across from me.

"They didn't pay for your treatment," he said. "I did."

"You did?"

"Before he died, my father left me a little money to cover his funeral. But I didn't want to spend the last thing I had of his on a casket and headstone. So it's been in this account, just sitting there... I didn't want you to think you owed—"

"Owe you? Why would I owe you anything?" Unsure how to react, I did what my instincts dictated I do and lashed out. "First, you lie to me. Then you dish my whole life story to the Stepford wives and all your other prissy, closed-minded followers. God knows what else you've done behind my back."

"You don't owe me a thing, Aida. But I did save your life, and whether that baby you're carrying is the Son of God or some stranger's offspring, forgive me if I feel invested in your situation."

"So, you don't believe me, then?" I was caught in a whirlwind of emotions—trying so hard not to cry that I was laughing.

"I am beyond proud of the progress you've made. But I'd be lying if I said I wasn't afraid." He stood up. "If the child is the product of an unfortunate mistake, I understand that. And I'm here for you. My true fear, though," he continued, "...What if it's not?"

As offended as I was by the priest's questioning of my character, his genuine concern floored me.

"What if," he said, "the child is exactly what you say it is? Are you prepared for what happens then?"

He was right. I wasn't. I didn't even know what would happen then.

"I've been reading the Bible," I said.

"Oh have you? Does that automatically qualify you to raise the second coming of Christ?"

I pulled out my phone and began to read a passage I had saved. "Corinthians... Um... *For he says, 'In a time of favor I listened to you, and in a day of salvation*

158

I helped you.' Behold, now is the time of favor; now is the day of salvation.'"

"And what do you think that means?" the priest challenged me. "Is God speaking to you through that?"

"I don't think he's speaking to me," I said. "I think it's about you."

WEEKS PASSED, and the priest made himself scarce to me. I'd see him at Mass, but he wouldn't hang out after, and he had a stand-in run the NA meetings for him. So, I stopped going, thinking that maybe he'd come looking for me this time.

The more I thought about it, the more the Bible verse made sense: The priest had prayed to God when he was in some type of trouble, *in a time of favor*, and God listened. God led him to me—so he could rescue me and help me realize my worth. While I didn't owe the priest anything, per se, I was waiting for my turn to help him. But I'd never been the patient type.

"I need a sign, God," I prayed. "What do I do now?" I waited and waited, but there was no answer.

Tired of talking to no one, I ventured out to do some grocery shopping. Even with another human budding inside of me, I felt more alone in public than I did at home. As I turned the corner of each aisle, I could feel people glaring at me, thinking, *Hmm...fat or pregnant?* I was hardly showing, but it's amazing what pregnancy can do to your body image— especially when you don't have family, friends, or a husband to tell you you're beautiful.

Without the priest to talk to, I felt abandoned. Now, he'd ghosted me, Mark wasn't answering my texts, and I was pacing through a supermarket hoping a stranger would say something reassuring out of the blue. Turning down the cereal aisle, I caught a glimpse of what appeared to be a familiar face—well, the back of a head, at least. It was my dad.

I rushed past all of my favorite cereals to follow him. Taking a sharp left toward frozen foods, I caught the heel of his boot in my peripherals. I raced around to the next aisle, and snapped my head around the corner to confirm the man's identity. But he was gone. I quickly walked to the front of the store to confront him on his way out. I waited there for ten minutes, and he never came.

Then, I took another lap around the entire store—up and down every aisle. Nothing. Had he seen me and run off? Was he checking up on me? Or, a better question: Was he real?

I ditched my cart in the middle of the store and left. Upon exiting the store, I surveyed the area—and there he was again: hands in his jacket pockets, crossing the street. I hardly looked both ways before darting through traffic. The man took a left down the next block, and then another quick left before entering a store.

As I approached the entrance, I saw it was a liquor store. Typical. I opened the door and stepped inside, breathing like I'd just run a marathon. The kid behind the counter watched as I nodded *hi* to him. He looked at me as if he'd never seen a visibly pregnant girl walk into a liquor store before.

If my dad was there, I knew exactly which aisle he'd be standing in. I made my way to the back of the store, where the whiskies resided. Sure enough, there he was. As I approached him from behind, I reached out to touch his shoulder.

"Hi there," the man said, turning his head around. "Excuse me." He grabbed a bottle off the shelf and squeezed past me. And like that, the childish fantasy that I had been chasing my father for twenty minutes disintegrated right in front of me. Disillusioned, I picked up a bottle of my dad's favorite scotch. Famous Grouse in hand, I headed for the counter.

14

CONFESSIONS

If we claim to have fellowship with him and yet walk in the darkness, we lie and do not live out the truth.
1 John 1:6

THE TRUTH is a concept that has consumed me for most of my adult life. I could never figure out which was more important: reality or what people believed to be real. The differences could be subtle but earth-shattering if discovered at the right moment. See, many people base their entire belief systems on what they believe to be true. That's faith. But what happens when the truth reveals itself and doesn't match up with the origins of that faith? Do people change their beliefs to better reflect reality, do they ignore the truth, or do they stop believing entirely?

I believe that, when well-intentioned, lies are mostly harmless. Some help people down paths they have already chosen subconsciously, while other lies prevent troubled individuals from putting themselves in further danger. Some lies hurt, yes. But others accomplish what even the truth cannot at times: comforting people.

As I sat in an AA meeting, listening to firsthand accounts of alcohol dependency, depression, and regret, I wondered how far I could stretch the truth to inspire these men to commit to change. I'd done it before, harmlessly—to motivate groups of people who sought hope. Because, without hope, what's the incentive to change?

"I know this needs to happen, for my family and myself," a man named Kevin finished telling his story, in tears. "I want to set a good example for my son and daughter. They shouldn't have to grow up with an unreliable father, and they definitely shouldn't be afraid of me when I drink."

"And you shouldn't be afraid of yourself, either," I added. "Thanks for sharing, Kevin." He nodded to me and sat back in his chair.

"You know, when I was working with children in Burundi," I began, "there was this young boy, Nabor. He didn't like his name, so we used to call him 'Nab' for short. Nab's father was a soldier in the Forces for National Liberation, a Hutu rebel group that had opposed the Burundian government for years. He died during a rebel attack on Bujumbura, leaving Nab, Nab's older sister, and his wife to fend for themselves. Nab's mother had begged the father time and time again to leave the Forces—and he knew, deep down, it was the right thing to do for his family. But he stayed and fought because he had a violent streak, and he was afraid of who he'd be—how that rage would manifest itself in a more traditional line of work. Would he act violently toward his family? For Nab's father, it was easier to put his life in danger than to deal with his problem head-on."

The room needed a second to digest the story. I got up and grabbed water from the refreshment table. Turning around to address the group, I noticed we had one more attendee than when we'd started: a young woman in the back with her hood up.

"Awesome story, Father. Really." I didn't expect to see Aida at a church meeting, let alone AA. "The boy you

164

talked about—Nab, was it? Where is he now? Is there a happy ending to this one?"

"Aida, what are you doing here?" I nervously scanned the rest of the group's faces to gauge reactions. Nobody knew what was going on. They didn't know Aida's story, or why a clearly pregnant woman would interrupt an AA meeting.

"I miss our talks," she slurred, standing up to approach me. "We don't talk. Why don't we talk anymore?" She reeked of alcohol.

"Aida," I grabbed her by the arm and took her aside. "Aida, are you drunk?"

AFTER CUTTING the meeting short and rushing the group out, Aida and I finally got to have our long-awaited talk. I politely asked her to remove her hood, and I had to confiscate a flask she'd stashed in her jacket pocket.

"Aida, do you know why I do these meetings?"

"Trust me," she said, "The irony of coming wasted to an AA meeting is not lost on me. And I hate drunks."

"Then what are you doing?"

"I actually wanna be able to be twenty-one. I didn't ask for this responsibility," she said, placing her palm over her stomach. "I did everything right for once, and this is how your God rewarded me."

"He's your God, too."

"Is it even ethical to sell booze to a woman who's obviously pregnant? The guy at the store didn't even ID me. Not so much as a 'Hey, who's this for?'"

She giggled through tears for a second before looking down at the floor. I desperately wanted to feel her anguish—but instead, I was awash with my own.

"I used to come to these meetings," I said. "Not to run them but as a member." Aida moved her eyes from her feet to my face. "My drinking was a major problem, but I found a way to move past it."

"How?"

"By stopping."

"Why?"

"Because I had to."

"No. *Why*?" she asked, incisively.

"I hurt somebody."

"What did you do? Hit a woman? Get in a bar fight? Forget to pick someone up from the airport?"

"No, Aida, I killed a child." My voice raised a bit.

Her eyes peered through me, like she was trying hard to believe me but couldn't. Following a slight pause, she responded, "Like, in Africa?"

"No. I've never been to Africa." As I spoke the words, I felt an immense weight lifted from my shoulders. That was the truth: I'd never been to Burundi. I'd never met a child named Nab, or helped build a well, or a school, or even donated money to a cause that did. Many of the things churchgoers thought I'd done were complete fabrications. The only reason I'd made them up was to inspire—and the only reason people listened to me was because I was a priest.

"A car accident. A young boy. I should've never gotten behind the wheel."

"When?"

"Almost five years ago."

Aida took a moment and looked around the room. Deep in thought, her eyes began to well up again. She quickly closed them, as if to trap the pain of being lied to inside.

"How the fuck did you keep this a secret? For five—"

"Aida, please sit down."

"No! How do they let someone like you become a priest? A spiritual leader, of a community that trusts you to guide them."

"My—"

"And their children?" She backed away from me. "What the fuck do you know about responsibility and 'the right path'? Are you even a real priest?"

"Of course! My faith has never been

disingenuous. My guidance has always come from the right place."

After the accident, I carried out my sentence—and my relationship with God only strengthened. You have a lot of time to reflect when you're incarcerated. And I had nearly two and a half years' worth of reflection. So, with nobody left on the outside—father passed away, mother long gone—my situation forced me to look inward. And that's where I found the most fulfilling answers.

"And where is that, 'the right place'?" Aida shook her head as I looked her in the eyes and pointed to my heart. "Why'd you decide to help me?" she asked.

"It was the right thing to do."

She didn't buy it.

"Okay." I paused and took a breath. "Because you gave me purpose."

I LANDED in Bujumbura around eleven o'clock Central African Time—which was four in the morning in Philadelphia. The seven-hour time difference had my brain in a scramble, unable to decipher the simplest directions in the airport, such as where to pick up my bags, where to meet my driver, and how to get to a restroom.

I was in Burundi for real this time, to educate and train pastors in a small town called Jimbi. By passing on my knowledge and passion for the gospel, I hoped to empower a new generation of preachers—vessels for the Word of our Lord. Armed with my faith and a few dozen Bibles, I was prepared to take on this new challenge with a gracious smile.

Jimbi was about a four-hour drive from the airport. There weren't many main roads to take, so it's not like we could've just hopped on another highway and found a quicker route. For a majority of the ride down, I enjoyed a beautiful view of Lake Tanganyika—a long freshwater lake that sat along the western coast of Burundi.

Sam, my driver, told me the lake's fascinating history, including an earthquake that had occurred when he was a child. Though the epicenter was on the west end of the lake, in the Congo, the tremors were felt all across East Africa. Sam remembered being in school at the time. The walls began to shake and tilt, and books slid off the shelves. His teacher quickly gathered the children and took them outside. But by the time everyone exited the classroom, the shaking had stopped. The kids didn't know whether to be scared or excited. That's what happens when you experience something potentially dangerous yet completely new.

I was in a similar situation. Burundi, though I'd told stories about it before, was foreign to me. I didn't know what to expect from my new life there, however temporary. Was I going to be okay? How could I be certain that I'd made a difference once I'd returned home? Would the people of St. Anthony's welcome me back with open arms?

I'd left the church in somewhat of a hurry, with little explanation, simply describing this missionary work as 'something I had to do.' The truth—the actual truth—was that Aida sort of blackmailed me into leaving. After our tense conversation, she gave me a long hug and said, "If you aren't out of here in the next two weeks, I'll tell the church what you did." Then she walked off.

She didn't know the church was already aware of my transgression. They knew me before the accident, and played a major role in my rebirth during my time in prison. But while the Archdiocese of Philadelphia knew my story, St. Anthony churchgoers did not—and that is who I wanted to keep the information away from. Losing credibility in their eyes would've been a knife directly into my chest. They may not have believed Aida if she told them, but she was right: I needed to leave.

I thought about her a lot in Africa, and kept her in my prayers every night. I hoped that, whatever the case was with her baby, that it would grow up healthy— and that she'd find purpose in caring for it. The more I contemplated it, the less likely it seemed that she was carrying the Second Coming of Christ. Even as a man of faith, the idea was far-fetched to me. Aida had appeared convinced, but the human mind is funny in that way. We'll convince ourselves of anything we want to be true.

Section Four:
Resurrection

———————

15

REBIRTH

MY SON was my son, and I loved him. He just looked... I knew he looked like me, obviously. He kind of had my nose. But there was something else about him that seemed familiar, and I couldn't pinpoint what it was. You know when you're watching a movie and you recognize one of the actors, and you know you've seen them before, but you can't remember where? It was like that, except there was no search engine or database for familiar baby faces.

I was fortunate, in a way. When my water broke, I was already at the hospital. I'd been experiencing sharp abdominal pain, and the doctor decided to keep me overnight. Sure enough, at three in the morning, the baby let me know it was time.

I'd heard my mom's retelling of my birth at least a hundred times. She usually left out all the gross details, but never short-changed the extreme agony I'd caused her throughout the long, arduous process. I always assumed she was exaggerating, playing up certain parts of the story to keep people's interest. But as I clenched in backbreaking pain on that hospital bed, I realized, if anything, she'd been underplaying the experience.

The feeling was extraordinary—just as a woman from work had described it: Your body wills itself to handle the pain because it knows you're bringing another life into this world. I suddenly understood why people described mothers as the strongest beings on the planet. For months leading up to that day, I doubted myself. I didn't think I could go through with having the baby. I wasn't strong enough. But I proved myself wrong.

During my second trimester, I was able to get a receptionist job at a lawyer's office. Lucky for me, the partners at the firm weren't looking for a college degree or tons of experience—and they agreed to hire me, knowing full well I'd be taking maternity leave within six months of starting the job. Both partners, Norman and Lacey, were very understanding. They were the closest thing I'd had to a support system. Since they assumed the father had walked out on me, all I got was sympathy and encouragement. They even sent chocolate and flowers to the hospital.

I never lied to them, though. It's not like I made up an intricate story about what happened to the baby's father. I'd simply say, "Oh, he's not around," or "He's not in the picture." And boom, no more questions—especially from Lacey.

The baby came three weeks early and was slightly underweight. I'd topped my mom's fabled account of my birth, in labor for nearly fourteen hours compared to her measly ten. Once the baby was out, I promptly passed out with a smile of relief on my face.

After a few hours of much-needed rest, the doctors woke me up in the gentlest, friendliest way possible. And that's when my eyes captured the most beautiful sight, one that I knew would change my life forever: my son, Evan.

WHEN I woke up in the hospital, I half-expected the priest to be waiting outside my room, like he had when I first met him. But he was nowhere to be found, and he was gone because of me.

I hadn't heard from him since I'd

barged in on an AA meeting, found out he was a murderer, and threatened him into leaving. Little did I know, he'd decided not to just leave the church, but to essentially flee the country—or so Zoe Roberson told me.

I was all too familiar with the concept of running away. My dad ran away from my family when I was a teenager. I've had friends run away from home, boyfriends ditch me and disappear from the face of the earth, and my mom's boyfriends completely abandon the both of us. But with the priest, it felt different. Yeah, I'd told him to leave, but it wasn't until after he left that I realized I might be completely lost without him.

The night I last saw the priest, I showed up at the church pretty buzzed—before he told me some devastatingly sobering things about him. I went there because I wanted answers. I wanted genuine companionship. I wanted to know I didn't have to go at this alone. I was almost three months pregnant at the time, my hormones were all fucked up, and I'd just chased the ghost of my father for like a mile into a liquor store. Maybe God wanted me there. Or maybe I was chasing a bunch of things I knew deep down I'd never catch.

I knew drinking was dangerous for

the baby, but after that night, I vowed never to put my child in harm's way again. If the priest wasn't going to be around to protect me from myself, I needed to reclaim control. All the time I'd spent alone helped me realize that it didn't matter if Evan was the second coming of Christ. I wouldn't be able to know that until he could walk and talk. So, until then, he was my son—and I was going to treat him like a loving mother treats her first child.

I spoiled the shit out of him. Someone had to. After all, he had one parent and no grandparents or other family in the picture. Using whatever money I could scrounge up, I bought him clothes and toys. Lacey was nice enough to give me an old crib she had in her house, from when her son was a baby. I did everything in my power to make sure Evan had a place to live, food to eat, and a parent that loved him.

Sometimes, when I was painting in the living room with Evan laying beside me, I'd see a man walk by the apartment slowly, almost as if he were trying to peek in the window. As much as I wanted to believe it was a familiar face coming to check up on the baby and me, I knew it may just as likely have been a stranger passing by.

EVAN WAS born on April 4. So, I celebrated the fourth of every month like it was his birthday. No balloons or cake, but we made it a party of our own. I danced with him, sang to him, put on his favorite movie. He may have had no idea what was going on, but he was such a smart baby.

In September, I took him for a nice walk down by the water. It was beautiful fall day—leaves scattered, sun shining, air crisp but not too cold. On our way back home, a bird shit on Evan's stroller, a gift I'd also gotten from Lacey. Though initially frustrated, I remembered that it was supposed to signify good luck.

When we got back home—after I'd wiped down the fortuitous stroller—I noticed a letter poking out of the mailbox outside our front door. Without thinking twice, I brought it inside and placed it on the counter. It didn't have a stamp or return address, and the envelope had my name written on it.

Curiously—but with caution—I began to open the unsealed envelope, peeking over at the baby every few seconds to make sure he was okay. I slid the letter out and unfolded it slowly. The handwriting looked vaguely familiar.

Aida, I'm sorry I left when
you needed me most.

That was it. No signature at the bottom, nothing else in the envelope. Could it have been the priest? Who else would've left me a letter?

If the priest was back in town, I knew he wasn't back at the church. Every couple of weeks, I would take Evan to Sunday morning mass at St. Anthony's. Some of the people recognized me—and I'd still get dubious looks from regulars like Carol, Susan, and Jodie. But the baby was mesmerized by the singing, and the organ, and the colorful stained-glass windows. Actually, church was about the only thing that would keep him quiet some weekends, so it was a nice break.

I hated to admit it, but St. Anthony's wasn't the same without the old priest. The new one wasn't as naturally engaging as the one I knew. This one mostly stuck to what was on the page, rather than freestyling and enlightening us with his own stories. Sure, the old priest's stories all turned out to be bullshit, but every single one had a worthwhile message. And at that point, you have to ask yourself which is more important: the truth of the story or the lesson behind it?

16

RETURN

The old things passed away; behold, new things have come.
2 Corinthians 5:17

TWENTY-TWO MONTHS came and went in Burundi. The experience was incredible. While I missed the St. Anthony's community I'd left behind, I found myself part of a new, budding Christian community in Jimbi. There, I didn't need to invent stories to inspire. The people were already impressed by who I was—for reasons I'll never understand—and they were already smitten with God's message.

My role, however, was not to preach.

It was to teach. But for me to do that effectively, I needed to first learn some things about myself—and my faith.

What had made my stories so powerful? Why did anyone at St. Anthony's listen to what I had to say, and how did I make them believe it? Why did some people come back every week, and why didn't others?

When I first started going to church regularly with my father, the message wasn't what captivated me. I found myself enthralled by the stories. Of course, the message was sometimes subtle, other times overt. But the narratives—the deep characters, the detailed settings, relatable conflicts, and immersive storytelling—those are what really fueled my interest. They kept me coming back every week. They galvanized me to purchase a Bible and read it on my own time. The stories monopolized my dreams before I even realized what some of their themes and messages were.

With an already-captive audience, all I needed to do was give them a reason to share the message they were so passionate about. Once they had purpose, I told them, they could go on to do great things—changing the lives of people in Jimbi, across Burundi, and someday, maybe even on the other side of the world. Instead of inventing a character to support my point, I simply used myself: a true story.

The townspeople loved me, and they enjoyed hearing about my experiences in America. When I'd first arrived in Jimbi, a few of the preachers-in-training gave me a nickname: *Umuzungu.* And I didn't find out until three weeks before I left that the word had meant 'white man.' They always giggled when they said it.

A young man named Elvis knocked on my door on my last Sunday in Burundi. *Kuwa imana* was 'God's day.' Elvis came to thank me for everything I'd taught him and the others—about preaching, about faith, and about life. He invited me to speak during an afternoon prayer service he was leading. I gladly obliged.

"WHEN I arrived here, I was terrified. I'd never been to Africa. I'd never been outside of the United States. In fact, I'd barely been out of the city of Philadelphia. But I came here with a purpose—a multi-layered one, at that. First of all, I wanted—I needed—to find myself. How was I going to do that? Through you," I said, looking out into a crowd of thirty-some-odd people. People I'd come to know, trust, and love over the course of the past two years.

"Through you all, I've located that point of light within myself again. The passion that burns for service, and faith, and kindness. The part of me that feels reinvigorated seeing someone else succeed. Or smile. And that was the second layer of my purpose here: to help you find the light that I believed, and now I know, exists in each and every one of you. To help you realize your dreams and spread God's Word to the people who need it most."

As I spoke, the crowd was silent, a majority of the young men nodding their heads in unison. There was a tangible stillness in the air—from the Burundi flag hanging behind me; to the quiet, deliberate breaths of the townspeople; to the gently swaying audience of trees in the distance.

"If you spread His message as widely as possible, you will reach many, many people. And I promise you, if you are able to help one person—just one—it's all worth it. That's all it takes. Change one person's life for the better. Inspire someone to treat others more kindly, to practice patience, to be more understanding. Just one. And you never know what you might learn in the process.

"I'd like to close this service with a quote from John 16:33: *In the world, you will have tribulation. But—"* One of the young men stood up. His name was Claude. As he stepped toward me, I didn't know what to expect.

"Urakoze, Umuzungu," he said. "Thank you," he clarified, in his broken English. Claude then pulled a banana leaf basket from behind his back and presented it to me. It was beautiful: hand-woven, with a leather strap and vibrantly colored diamond patterns decorating the outside. *"But take heart,"* continued Claude, *"I have overcome the world."*

I had nothing to add. My friend Claude had solidified the reason I'd ventured to Burundi in the first place. He showed me that people were willing to learn, so they could take that knowledge and inspiration to help others. And that was all the vindication I needed. "Genda n'amahoro," I said to the crowd, holding back tears of elation. *Go in peace.*

The service evolved into a night-long ceremony, filled with Burundian music and dancing—a joyful sendoff. I taught Elvis how to dance like his namesake, rattling his knees back and forth on beat with the drums. A group of men taught me the *intore*, a traditional Burundi warrior dance performed with weapons, often to celebrate weddings and funerals.

I would've loved for the dancing to

have continued forever, but finally it was time for me to return home.

I THOUGHT about calling Aida when I got back from Burundi. But I didn't know what to say. I considered writing her a letter, even something simple like 'I'm sorry' or 'Hope you're doing well.' But I couldn't bring myself to. Nothing I did or said would have made a difference—the damage was done, and I wasn't sure our relationship could ever be repaired.

Our connection, though organic, was founded on pain and personal turmoil. It wasn't friendship; it was a Band-Aid.

Cathartic, yes. Genuine, certainly. But our bond wasn't designed to last, just to patch up what was already broken. And maybe that was fine. We tore off the bandage and were doing any remaining healing on our own.

In life, people come and go. When you have a pleasant conversation with a stranger on the train or at the grocery store, you don't exchange numbers and hope to see that person again. You accept the experience for what it was and move on.

Of course, other encounters are deeper than that. Some turn into relationships that last months, years, or even a lifetime. And though all relationships eventually end—whether through death or otherwise—getting to know Aida and sharing that bond with her was important, something that I knew would stick with me.

I wondered a lot about the baby and how they were doing. Aida didn't necessarily need the father to help raise it; I just hoped she wasn't doing it alone. Now that the child had been born, the question of who the father was seemed less important. But it still tortured me.

There were two possibilities: Either Aida lied, or she didn't. And somehow, neither seemed likely.

Recalling every word of every conversation we'd had—from the hospital all the way up to the AA meeting—I racked my brain for some type of clue. I'd seen her recovery crush, Dr. Monterro, in all his glory at the rehabilitation center. I knew she had at least one close male friend her age. There could have been other men in her life I didn't know about.

Hell, she could have even been repressing the encounter that led to the pregnancy, if it'd been traumatic enough. But the timeframe didn't add up. Could somebody have forced himself upon her at the center? If that was the case, would she have told me about it? Would I have noticed her shift in mood over the phone?

188

This train of thought made me realize: Maybe I didn't really know Aida. Maybe I didn't know her in the same way she didn't really know me. I'd told her to stop assuming we were so different, when in reality, I had no right to assume we were any bit the same.

During my incarceration—my forced rehabilitation—I had many enlightening conversations with my cellmate. He taught me the importance of owning the conversations you have with yourself.

You have a lot of free time in prison. Time to contemplate, doubt, wonder, punish yourself with 'what if's. Since the conversation is entirely internal, the onus is on you to keep it going. Mental silence is the enemy—it's driven far stronger men than me insane.

But all that pressure to think can send your thoughts in directions you'd rather them not go. You end up asking a lot of questions—questions you think you want the answers to, but answers you know you'll never find fully satisfying.

Am I a bad person? Do I belong here? Do I deserve this? Why did I do it? What could I have done differently? Am I capable of change? Do I want to?

When you allow your mind to wander and find yourself down a path that's harrowing to explore, it's critical to have a way to pull yourself back.

I'll never forget this advice, which my cellmate said he'd learned from his lawyer while on trial: "If you don't like the answer, change the question."

"CAN YOU name a Bible verse for me?" I asked a young man sitting in my favorite pew.

"Uh, John 3:16?" Sure enough, he gave me the answer I was looking for.

"That's right. John 3:16 is the most famous verse—what, with those signs at baseball and football games, and plenty of people have tattoos of the name and number. But how many know what the verse actually says?

"Do you?" I said, looking to Tom Roberson. He shook his head. "You?" I asked Susan Bilken. "How about you?" I motioned to Tom's son Jacob.

"It says that God loves us, so he sacrificed His only Son," said Jacob. "And if we believe in Him, we'll go to Heaven." Everybody laughed. Clearly he'd been paying attention in CCD.

"You're not wrong, Jacob. But it's funny how 3:16 is so popular, and we often forget what John writes next: *For God did not send His Son into the world to condemn the world, but so that the world might be saved through Him.*"

I gave people a chance to absorb the words and digest their meaning.

"Jesus wasn't here to judge us. He was here to make us better people. And when He comes again, that will be true again."

One could argue that the idea of someone coming to judge us contributes to our improvement as people. So, in a sense, believing Judgment Day is imminent could directly lead to positive change. But there will always be folks who do the opposite. If they believe the world is ending, they cease to give a damn. They don't need someone else to judge their actions because they've already judged themselves, and the verdict wasn't good.

As I returned to the altar, I heard a man whisper-yell the name *Evan* from behind me. Curious, I quickly turned around to see a child no more than two years old running down the aisle. He sat with a bearded man who looked to be his grandfather. I took a seat in the celebrant chair as it dawned on me: I recognized the boy's face.

But it couldn't be. I hoped to never relive that valley of my life, and though I see his face every night when I'm staring at the ceiling praying for sleep, the boy was still there at Mass—even when I blinked. This time, it was real. It was the same face I'd studied in milliseconds, with time slowed, as I caused the crash that flipped a family's world upside-down.

I blinked again. Upon opening my eyes, I caught another familiar face walking down the aisle. It was Aida.

Fatalistically, I laughed to myself as we shared a smile, and she joined the young boy and older man in the pew.

The night I found Aida, I was the lowest I'd been in years. It's true that without me, she probably wouldn't be alive—and with a purpose. But the reverse is also true. Maybe she's the one who saved me.

ABOUT THE AUTHOR

Ryan Hussey is a seasoned copywriter who writes
fiction and non-fiction in his spare time. His work
has been featured in *Essig Magazine*, Elite Daily,
Thought Catalog, and The Good Men Project.
Ryan also manages an online publication called
The Bigger Picture and has written short stories that
include "Telle Mère, Telle Fille" and the serial
fiction project "Dr. Jeremy."